The More
We Are Together

stories

OITE

Gift of
Fr. John R. Cavanaugh,
C.S.B.

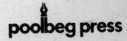

poolbeg press

First published 1980 by
Poolbeg Press Ltd.,
Knocksedan House,
Swords, Co. Dublin, Ireland.

Cover photograph by Liam White
Designed by Steven Hope

The generous assistance of An Chomhairle Ealaion (The Arts
Council) in the publication of this book is gratefully
acknowledged.

Printed by Cahill Printers Limited,
East Wall Road, Dublin 3

Some of these stories first appeared in *The Bell*, *Irish Writing*, and *The Irish Press* 'New Irish Writing'.

Contents

The American Apples

The only plants she had grown before were geraniums. They blossomed for her the way cats purr for spinsters. I can't recall the names of the varieties but I remember the blossoms: the one that was a crimson stray—away from elegance and somehow a stranger to all but herself in the place, the pinks with a blush that set with the sun on the youth of our grandmothers, the purples, the red that was a rose without smell and the white that smelled like a veil away for years in lavender. I know with what prim docility they grew for her in greying earth in sweet tins brought from shops to the sills of the rooms in New Lane where we lived.

As an altar boy I went often on to the High Altar of the Cathedral when the priest away below in the pulpit droned the last prayers of Holy Hour. I would fit the long lighted taper into the brass tube on the cone cowl of the extinguisher and light the hundreds of candles, from the Tabernacle all the way down red-carpeted steps to the patterned tiles of the Sanctuary. Every cluster of candles I lit raised a richness of flowers out of stained-glassed dusk. Flowers from the hot-houses of the earl and the agent and the manager and the doctor; in root and on stem they were there in their thousands, smelling like cool incense, but never was there a geranium in the lot that was better than my mother's.

Even that the sweet-tins had discreet burial there in urns of beaten brass and bronze I used to recognise her few flowers when my butterfly flame hovered over them, holding their own with the best.

So when the old man laughed on the day of the apples, I let laughter alone while she prised the pips from the hearts with her nail: no hard task because the brother and I had gnawed our way to the core. They were sleek, cider-wry yellow apples, freckled where they had out-bowed leaf shade on the branch.

She was sitting on the edge of the chair near the hearth. The hat she had brought, after fourteen years in Boston to her wedding, flaunted the wear and tear in fur felt with one defiant feather. The black nap of the coat that travelled with it wore a silver clip in the right lapel for the same reason. The ten years since she was twenty-five showed in her heart-shaped face only in a slight slackness of flesh below her chin.

The brother sat cross-legged on the floor looking up at her. I too sat on the floor between a basket of groceries and two heads of cabbage. The old man stood over us, hat at angle, thumb hooked to

6

the watch pocket of his waistcoat.

While she had shopped he was detailed to have an eye on the brother and me in that one of two rooms near the slates of a two-storey tenement, and his ear had been at full cock for her step on the cobbles. Tap-a-tap-tap she came, eighteen to the dozen down the lane, in the hall and up the stairs. He drew on his hat, poked for pipe and plug, and felt for coin in pants pockets, but by then she was in at the door. One in each hand she held the apples, the basket on her arm and the cabbages cuddled by her elbows.

'Look what I got for the boys,' she said, a bit breathless, her eyes making more of the gift than was usual.

'Apples!'

'More, boys!'

'What, woman,' asked the father.

'American apples!' she said.

'Only that you told us, they could be out of Pat Carty's sour half-acre in Ballydribeen,' the old man joked.

'Here Michael, here Kevin,' she said, and then put her load on the floor.

'Eat them,' she urged, before we had a tooth in them.

'God, I thought we were to have them under a glass globe with a lamp burning in worship of their highnesses,' the old man said.

'I'm not rushing ye, boys,' she told us, 'but I'm going to keep the seeds and save them till 'tis spring again. I'll save the seeds.'

'And save your soul,' mocked the old man.

7

'If saving seeds would save a soul I'd have to rob an orchard for yours.'

'A Boston orchard.'

'One tree out of a Boston orchard would do.'

'No, woman, mine is one Irish soul that's not for sale in American dollars.'

'I brought my soul home with me, and some dollars too,' she snapped.

When she held the seeds in her palm the old man laughed. Moving to the door, he ballad-sang:

'The Yanks are coming.
You can hear them humming
Over there . . .'

She pretended not to hear as she put the seeds in an envelope and put the envelope between the Sacred Heard picture and the warmth of the hob.

'Over there. Neither here nor there,' mocked the old man in doorway.

'When spring comes we'll see,' she called after him as he went to slake a summer thirst.

The lane gave spring no easy coming amongst us. Flowering weeds had laboured birth in old mortar along old walls. Grass stems over-reached in lankness so that bright green tips might show between and above the slug-backed cobbles. House-bound old people had to wait for their cage-bound birds to sing again before they could be sure that they had weathered another winter. But ahead of weed and grass and finch song, she took the seeds from hob-warmth. Next morning she took a distemper tin with her to her usual first

Mass at the Friary. Coming home, she reached through the Friary railings for fists of earth from a flower-bed. Then on she came with another tin-full of monastery garden for her sills.

She waited until the hour between the father's going to work and ours to school before she brought tin and seeds together on the sill. School bags on hip, the brother and I watched her prod four holes in the earth with one of the old man's chisels and drop a seed into each hole.

A murmur of mist soothered on the lane. Rain beads roped and broke along the rusty shute above the open window.

'A wonderful day to plant seeds, but bad for the pay-packet if it gets any more rainy, so you don't know where you are,' she told us. 'A stone set in damp, sweats for years after, whereas a seed set in mist is set in growth, they say. Ye remember ye said the apples were nice tasted?' We said we did.

'Were they real sweet?'

'Sweet with a tang.'

'And juicy?'

'Oh, yes.'

'Remember how they looked myself. Yellowy-goldy and marked like blackbirds' eggs. Maybe from these four seeds four trees of them will grow. The ways of God are wonderful.' She looked from the tins to us and back to the tins again. 'I wonder are they that wonderful?' Then, wide-eyed, she looked at me and said 'Oh, God forgive me.'

'We can say a prayer,' Kevin encouraged in all earnestness and her laughter raced up and down and up its scale. Then, suddenly serious herself,

9

she said: 'School now; off to school; school is important.'

'I wonder do I know about that looney Cromwell's killings all over the country?' Kevin asked, scratching behind an ear.

'We can say a prayer,' she mimiced, laughing again. 'But you do, Kevin,' she added, all concern. But Kevin's sleepy-headed solemnity was too much for her. Her laughter followed us down the stairs. When we reached the lane her serious face was waiting over the sill of flowers for us.

'Kevin, Cromwell happened in sixteen-something. He was a bad man, but the strange thing was that when he had slaughtered hundreds of people he—'

'I know,' Kevin interrupted. He gave her one of his slow-fashion grins. 'He said a prayer.'

The three of us laughed that time. Then Kevin butted his thick thatch into the mist with the two steps he always held ahead of me. I listened to her laughter gentling over the planted seeds and wondered idly whether a thing would grow from them.

I don't think she wondered though. So far as I know she never wondered where her gift for growing things came from. She was bred of a lane like our lane, daughter of a stone-mason, married to a stone-mason bred of a lane that like ours was wrought of stone, paved with stone that let nothing of root thrive on it but lichen and moss and nothing between but the weed and the striplet of grass. In fact our lane's very bareness may have been a reason why she wanted us out of it, but certain it is that she wanted Kevin and me to stay longer in school than our kind, to have Boston at home, no less, and she had an idea that a lane was a bad start for that.

Two years from the morning of the seeds she had us a walk distant from town in a stone house that had two cat-swings of flower plot in front, a crusty quarter-acre of one-time commonage to pass for garden at the back. How that came about is another story. But in the way the peacock-feather and the silver clip had more to be defiant about everyday.

But a bank manager had been persuaded that a meagre-enough warren of dollars would bed and breed issue with docile rows of shillings kidnapped on the roll from a four-pound pay packet to butcher, baker, grocer, tailor and the old man's pocket on Saturday pay-day, when there was pay. Urban councillors were persuaded that the manager was persuaded that the old man was convinced that the age of miracles was not dead.

The old man argued, angered, mocked and then laughed the way he did about the seeds. But it was on the night that we left the lane for the house in the country that he had reason to remember the seeds again.

Daylight for the flitting would be merciless on the few sticks of furniture, she thought, and her hopes were answered by an October night without moon or stars. In a rumble of iron-shod wheels Mick Breen's dray lantern rocked down the lane like a buoy-light in an inshore harbour. The shoes of his Clydesdale chipped flint sparks big as match-spurts off the cobbles. The old man's face loomed bronze-like in the museum half-glow of the lantern before Mick knew who he had and where he was.

She helped the lantern with her hob-lamp in the doorway while the old man gave Mick a hand. The old man held the lamp while she fetched the geraniums tin by tin for careful placing in a packing case at the back of the dray. When the last geranium was in place and she faced for the house he asked her: 'What now?'

'You'll see,' she told him.

Mick put me sitting on a folded sack under a sleek slope of the horse's rump and put the lantern in my grip. 'The heat of it will keep you warm,' he told me. He himself sat opposite, with Kevin in the old man's timber armchair, in line with the horse's tail, between us. With her footsteps in the hall came the old man's question:

'And what the hell might they be, woman?'

'Two Boston apple trees to save your soul.'

'Well, I'll be damned.'

'Not if you don't decide to leave us before these two little plants that grew are trees.'

'Put them in the ould box with the flowers.'

'Indeed I will not.'

'Then what'll you do, woman?'

'Why, carry them myself, of course.'

'Not with me, you won't.'

'Then I'll have to walk alone.'

'You damn well will.'

She was standing in the doorway with the tins held against her body. He was facing her with the hob-lamp still lighting in his hand.

'It will be a poor journey to the new house if I

12

have to walk alone to it,' she said.

'Then dump the ould weeds out of my sight,' he said.

'They're not weeds. They're only stems with a few leaves now but they'll be trees one day.'

'All right, put 'em in the box.'

'No,' she insisted, and as if to ease over the firm finality of the word she added: 'They had the courage to grow in the old house so 'twould be a shame if anything happened them before they saw the new house.'

'Their ould lad saw the new world, isn't that enough?' he jibed, but you could tell that he was near the end of patience. Her answer did not help either.

'They're going to a new world now. I'm taking them there myself.'

'What!' he cried, and on the word she tried a pleasantry.

'A wonder the lamp wouldn't help you to see light.'

She could hardly have said a more unsuitable thing. Suddenly made aware of the lamp he saw how ridiculous he looked.

'To hell with the light,' he cried, swinging the lamp arm violently. The lamp arced over the dray and quenched in a globe-burst against the blank wall opposite. The horse heaved forward. The dray rattled my teeth together. I had a glimpse of the mother following on with the tins before I had to look ahead for balance on the jigging perch. Sound of the wheels must have been listened for by the neighbours. Door after door to lane's end opened.

13

Families called out of kitchen glow of light and warmth 'God go with ye, good luck, safe home!'

When I could venture to look back I saw her and the old man walking together through doorway light. She was bowing and smiling like a celebrity on parade. He was carrying the seedlings in their tins.

On more and roomier sills of windows more generous with light she tended her tin-can garden throughout the winter, but I think that from Christmas onward she watched through the windows for the spring. Back of the house she saw fields swell in a green wave to foam along the sky-line into firs. The air was full of free birds' wings. The air itself felt free, it seemed to have hinted to her about spring even before the trees or the fields or the birds showed awareness of it. Anyhow she was out one morning in the back plot with a digging fork where there was a skim of frost tinselled in sun that had only lit to boast about.

Again it was in that hour between the old man's departure for work and ours for school. Small-spare in the quarter acre she picked at the hard earth like a robin at a crust in the school yard. Her palms let down her will-power in that first day but she had done enough for the old man to notice the bird scratch on the alligator hide of our domain. He was always suspicious of her motives in these displays of industry, especially in departments where he felt she must have known how futile her own attempts must be. He never could decide how much honest effort went into the work and how much was stage-setting for intimidation to stalk

14

on and leer up at his place in the gods.

To be on the safe side he staged a show of his own: champing, tossing his head at the roof, roaring murder to the rafters, then blaspheming his way to a door-bang exit for the fork to the toolshed to dig between dinner and dark of that evening—and every evening after he pick-axed and forked in that plot till the crows flapped home to their rookery-ring of beeches. So when spring came down the hill of fields she was there in the torn earth, intimidating with a young tree in each hand, the empty distemper tins beside the cast-off work-boots of the old man.

I can't recall how many springs went by before the men of the house realised that the way of God with trees was wonderful after all. She had known before us that her forlorn-looking hopes had bole and branch and leaf. Her worry had been that never in any spring had the trees held blossoms and never in autumn were there apples to pick. Every spring she had watched, but for every summer there were only leaf for every autumn to wither.

Her garden otherwise was all that a garden should be. Cabbages, carrots, parsnips, radishes, rhubarb, thyme; currants like drops of claret and sherry and currants black as pitch blobs; gooseberries green and bitter, gooseberries red and amber and kind; raspberries, strawberries, melons and parsley thronged from the earth to her. All of them travelled with her in baskets to market to keep the shillings rolling dollarwards in the bank for the house. The shilling that came home with her travelled back on other days to pay for each term of mine as a day-boy in the town's seminary and out of town once a week to Kevin, who had got a scholarship to a college a train-day journey up country.

Hardly a root stirred in the earth without her knowing. Cat-like she watched for weeds and pounced on them, bearing them away by the apron-full to dump under the privet hedge where cats slumbered with one eye awake for other quarry. With the slumbering cats' quietness of pleasure she saw the colour of the crops richen between soil and stalk and stem and leaf. But always, I think, there was one dreaming eye on the apple trees, and year by year the dream was chilling in it.

Then one Saturday afternoon, when the garden was prostrate in autumnal dying and the trees humped in a tattered shroud of withering, the old man stood at the kitchen back window looking out at them, kindling his pipe, smoke oozing about the hat he had on for the road to a pub with pay-day substance. Without moving his gaze from the garden he said: 'I see the Yanks are yet to come?'

The flat-iron slowed to a stop on his shirt for Mass in the morning. Still looking at the kitchen table top she said with careful carelessness: 'I know that well.'

'I wonder is it how the haggart isn't grand enough for 'em?'

'The trees weren't too grand to grow in it.'

'Like hens without eggs, only we could eat the hens.'

'And use the trees for firing,' she countered.

'Green burning,' he gave back, going to the front

door. 'Is there anything you want from town?'

'You home early and sober,' she told him.

He laughed and closed the door. She finished her ironing without a word, cleared the table and then went to look out the window. I was greasing the leather of a football boot out of washboard curl and stiffness.

'I wonder why the trees don't bear fruit, Michael?' she asked me without turning.

'I don't know,' I said.

With that the old man returned to the doorway.

'Do you know where Tommy Cronin lives, Mick? I couldn't know his pub because he never takes a wet, but you knock around with his son?'

He went when I told him where Tommy lived. I wondered at his closing the door as if there was a child to wake with the sound of the lock. But in the feel of the silence he left after him I knew why. She was at the core of it, and my gaze was drawn by it to her. Her stillness might have had no breathing in it, so still she stood, yet the silence it summoned to her had unease. Hers was the blank back of a woman in a moment when she relinquishes yet another illusion to leak away from her in tears. When she turned there were no tears but I caught her un-awares by the look I had not time to take away from her. She winced at it, recovered instantly, but what she meant for a smile of not-caring ended in one of never-mind.

Without a word she went through the pantry into the yard. I heard her poking in the tool-shed. I took a turn at the window myself, in time to see her walk up the centre path of the garden toward

17

the apple trees, standing together in an oval green patch half-way up. Her hands were held in front of her. Her back had lost anonymity now, as when the belief relinquished makes room for a belief less easy to give home to. She looked who she was, but not quite what she had been, somehow.

When she was some paces from the oval she paused for an instant, then she walked on purposefully and went sidewise on her knees beside the right-hand tree. With a sweep she rasped the teeth of a saw through tender bark to blossom-white pith of the young tree and sawed till the shock head bowed inch by inch, to collapse in a sigh of near-spent leaves onto the ground. When she stepped over the stump toward the comrade tree I felt I should persuade her to stop, without quite knowing why. I was in the act of moving when she paused in the act of kneeling. She straightened slowly and looked intently from the lowest to the highest branch of that remaining tree. Then she let the saw fall from her hand, stood on for another moment and walked back quickly towards the house.

I schooled my impulse to look up from the boots when she arrived in the kitchen. Between the laying of a saucer and a cup she paused.

'I cut one of the trees, Michael,' she said. Before I could comment she ran on with 'I was going to cut the other but I felt that the patch would be bare without something in it.' She paused again, the pause of an instant, then she added: 'Wouldn't that be the thing?'

'Just so,' I said, without any inflection whatever.

There was a longer pause then, as if my saying of

my say left the situation wholly hers again.

'What would you like for tea, Michael?' she asked me suddenly, and I felt as if she were home from a journey.

That evening, on plea of a football club meeting, I got away to fourpenny hop in the Old Town Hall. The evening felt as if winter was near enough to have chilled it with the breath of cold that I could feel at the open neck of my shirt. I had gone several hundred yards when I heard her calling my name. When I turned she was running towards me with my mackintosh. The manner of her running made me see how worn-out-of-time she was going. The heart shape of her face was that of an old heart now and in the folds of loose flesh under her chin I could see the pulse-beats of an old heart floundering in her breathlessness.

'Those meeting rooms are draughty, Michael, and there is quite a cold out this evening. Better wear your coat.'

I was about to refuse it when I remembered I had in mind to lure a harpie from the dance and that the coat would be handy. I took the coat.

'Good-bye now, Michael,' she said as if we had not met for a year and would not meet again for another.

On her way back to the house she paused to wave to me but after the second occasion I looked back no more.

The harpie delayed me longer than I bargained for, and I walked home under a mooned midnight, bright as a wan-gone noon. The key was in the front-door lock and I let myself into the hall without a sound. My hand was on the kitchen light-switch when I saw her shape between me and the smouldering fire.

I switched on the light. With what had been a rich blue dressing gown, gold roped on the edges—the last remaining item of her American trousseau—now gone to fadedness, she sat slippered in the old man's armchair in front of the fire. She turned to look at me intently, her hair hanging loose about her face from a shoe-string on her nape.

'Michael, this is no hour for a seminary boy to come home. What would the priests say if they knew of it?'

'The meeting was heated and lasted longer than anyone thought,' I lied.

'Besides, 'tis after twelve and you can't have supper, going to Communion in the morning.'

'I'm not hungry,' I said.

'And your father has not come home yet. Drinking money that we could do with to hold house and home where he is the only wage-earner, while I run myself to rags to keep up appearances in ye. 'Tis at the point now that one week of idleness for him and disaster faces all my hopes.'

The banging of the front gate and a lurched step signalled the old man's coming in his cups. Slurring of footsoles on concrete told of effort to find balance before facing the four steps and the pathway to the door.

'Come quickly. Leave the light on or he'll brain himself. If he finds you here there'll be questions about where you were.'

She pulled me by the arm after her up the stairs.

We were hardly on the landing before he fell in at the door. She held me until he had picked himself up, telling himself to steady up, let there be no panic, woman and children first and God for us all. Without question of the light in the kitchen he side-stepped into it in a half keel-over that ended in the slap of his palm against the hob to keep from falling again. When the chair-joints screeched under his sudden weight she relaxed her grip on my wrist. She firmed it again in reassurance, put a finger to her lips and tip-toed to her room. I followed suit to mine.

Moonlight through the open window had transformed it into a place of grace like a mendicant's cell. A moth fluttering upstream towards the moon's face was ivory white as a prayer of grace under way might be. When I thought of the harpie, the thought felt like a stain but I brought it with me to the ivory moth in the moonlight and looked out the window. I felt I was fighting that pure fierce light with my life for re-possession of a room that had been mine, and that the harpie was merely a spectator at the struggle, leering-luring with her eyes for my eyes under a loop of her oil-heavy hair. Moonlight was focussed direct upon the earth, with such intensity that the butt of the cut tree showed like a bleached wound in the withered garden.

A chair crashed in the kitchen and the old man's unsteady steps sounded through the pantry. The back door banged open. The steps stumbled across the yard and presently I could see him hatless at the garden gate. Up the centre path he went, his head huddled in his left shoulder-blade, his left hand straight out, like a punch-drunk has-been of the ring reliving in perpetuity the moment before the final crash to canvas. When he was four paces from the trees he stopped in his tracks. After a long pause the outstretched hand counted one-two, one-two where the comrade trees should have been: then one, and one again it counted, then it wove a nought over the fallen tree. He was talking aloud but I could not hear what he was saying.

He blundered up to the rooted tree and gripped a branch. Holding on with one hand he groped in his pocket with the other. What he removed from the pocket was recognisable when the two hands came to play on it and a blade flashed for an instant in the moonlight. His pocket-knife. Head down he butted through the lower branches of the tree to the bole. Then round the bole slowly, carefully he groped, his right hand obviously working on it all the time.

When he had come full circle he shadow-boxed down the garden to the house again, face swollen, eyes glazed, to make the punch-drunk likeness nearer true than ever. Through the house he barged without closing a door; up the stairs and into their room.

'What the hell happened up there?' he shouted in the room doorway.

'Up where?' she asked, coolly and firm.

'Woman, I said!!'

'What now?'

'That tree!'

'Oh, I cut it down with the saw.'

'What did you do that for?'

'Why shouldn't I?'

'Why should you?'

'Up to now 'twas you supplied all the reasons for that. The Yanks are coming. Dump the old weeds. A hen without eggs.'

That last gave him pause. Sufficient for her to run in explanation: 'Trees without fruit have no place in that garden. Fruit would sell and we need all we can sell with our purse the way it is and our commitments the way they are.'

'Was that what you were thinking when you saved the seeds and planted 'em?'

'Times have changed.'

'And who the hell changed 'em?'

'I did. And 'tis up to me to see to it, as far as I can, that the change is for the better.'

'By God, 'tis mighty practical you got of a sudden.'

'I'm practical now, yes.'

'Full-blown practical.'

'Yes, I have to be.'

'Then why didn't you cut down the second tree?'

After a pause she said: 'Come to bed and don't disgrace us with that shouting.'

'I'll shout all I like, when I like, how I like and where I like.'

'Come to bed.'

'Listen, woman,' he shouted, 'leave that second tree.'

I lay on the bed for a while, hearing his voice drone on in querulousness, then drowsiness, then it was lost into silence and snoring. I went down to close the doors. At the back door, curiosity got the

23

better of me and I went up the garden to the apple tree. A band of bark was cut with surprising neatness from the bole at the point where he had used the knife. I wondered why. Then I remembered that the Tommy Cronin he had enquired about last evening was by way of being a gardener.

From that I guessed correctly that, by what seemed to me like rule of thumb, he had performed a grafting operation on the barren tree. I never told him I knew about it. She neither knew nor noticed that it had been done.

She had other things to occupy her mind. Christmas ended the best of winter in beginning a period of idleness for the old man. She dreaded idleness for many reasons, he for one special reason, his inability to live without working. Signing at the Labour Exchange hurt his dignity in craft and taking the palm-full of silver every Friday seemed to him like cadging, doing Judas on his principles.

He would return from signing with a paper in his pocket and read slowly through patched-up spectacles, rising to pace the kitchen, window to window, when his eyes got tired of a combination of bad glasses and unlovely print.

Noticeable in particular was the restlessness of his squat strong hands. Again and again he would anchor them with his thumbs to his leather belt but always they broke free to poke for a pipe he could not light that often on short tobacco, to grope in trousers pocket for coin that was not there, to punish each other's leathern palms with prominent knuckles or plunder a match box for stems to chew to ease his craving for tobacco. His

24

hands seemed to live a life of their own in a period like that. They were of him but not quite with him, like gun-dogs fidgeting about the master's heels on a day when hills held promise for the hunt.

She made much to-do with little and less to do with. She whipped lean meals to lively meal-times with rush and bustle in the making. Her bustle irritated him because he was missing the customary pint off the neck of the bottle before drawing his chair to table. His careful pacing between the windows irritated her because it seemed to knell the futility of her make-believe when the meals were met by hunger. They snapped at each other when their minds met, then they stood on opposite sides of a palpable silence. Buff bank envelopes cut with elegant edge to the heart of the matter at intervals. Then the wedding-present silver and the mantel clock and her American gold watch travelled with her to the pawn shop. In the lane she would have had her dollars to draw on. In crop time she would have had baskets for market. Now there was an arid garden and in the centre a barren tree.

Until spring. Spring's first flowering showed on her geraniums. Tending them eased odd hours for her between house chores and questing visits to chapel. Spring brought the fork to the old man's hands and they drove it into the earth, with a will for the job that in time of craft they had done with contumely. Spring brought sun to the sills, song to the silence, growth to the soil and leaves to the apple tree.

Spring brought her into the garden to plant while he prepared the ground ahead of her. In the first

25

days she looked at the leafing tree when she entered the garden. She did that every day, until the third or fourth day after leafing was complete, and the tree looked as if it had given all it could to the year and was content. I can say that with certainty because, in guise of study at the window of my room, I brooded on how I was going to ease over to her the fact that I was not going on for the priesthood; my reason for going to the seminary in the first place and her strongest wish.

I was at the window on the morning that the tree had blossom for the sun, a white froth of blossom broken by the leaves so it looked like the lace on a surplice, a garland for a bride, a quilt for a marriage bed.

The old man had seen it first because he was in the garden before I came to the window. She came into the garden with an apron of seed potatoes, dragging the loose boots. Propped by the handle of the spade in his armpit the old man watched her as she moved along the drill spacing the seed, her cloth-bound head bowing towards the tree. Seeing me at the window the old man nodded at the tree and beckoned me down. When I arrived in the garden her unconsciously ceremonial, ritual-like bows in the spacing of the seed had brought her blue-clothed head under the white blossom. She put seed in the last place, put her hands on the small of her back to help her straighten. Her head touched a branch of blossom as it raised, then the branch flicked before her like a wand and she was looking at the transformed tree. Her body tensed. She stood staring at the tree without expression for several seconds. Then 'Oh, oh, oh,' she whispered. Then hardly above a whisper 'Oh, oh, oh God, isn't it lovely!'

Her face broke on all its lines into a smile. Her eyes brightened slowly from glow to real brightness. The left-over potato seed dropped on her boots and she was walking into the tree. She walked right on into the bole. She cupped her palms about the slim stem.

'Michael, Dad! Look at my tree, look at my tree!' she called.

'The Yanks are here at last,' said the old man.

'Oh, God, isn't it lovely?' she cried.

With a smile she emerged out of the tree looking straight at the old man.

'Now didn't I tell you I would have a fruiting tree,' she said.

He said: 'Wonders will never cease,' then he began to smooth the earth over the drill of new-set potato seed. Before she could turn her smile towards me I walked down the garden, away from both of them.

The Old Stock

It was the last thing we owned in that town: the well field. In law and in daylight it belonged to the two Leary brothers but they were two of us. Two of the old stock in that town that used to be ours. Through them and with them in daylight we owned the well field. By night it neither belonged to us nor to the two Leary brothers. By night it belonged to the ghosts of our people: the ghosts of the old stock. And even by night we were nearer to the well field than were the new people who were the new owners of our town, because the old stock living this life were near to the old stock living that other life the length of a last breath away.

We were craftsmen those of us who were born with that feeling for the grain in green stone, the vein in sweet timber, the glow in the heart of dark iron, the gloss in the hide of dull leather, the white lightness in grey troughs of dough. Those of us in whom the feeling for these things was dulled by the will of God or the blood of mothers not of our kind were skilled tenders of craftsmen.

We were quiet men, quiet-spoken in the week-days. Our work-hour concentration relaxed at home into the comfort of unlaced boots, the ease of old wooden chairs with long arms and straight backs that braced the ache in tired spines until the specs fell from the bone of the nose and the news-paper was crushed between thighs and the weight of hands. Then our wives came from their mending for a moment to put the specs where our boots when we walked out of sleep would not crush them.

And while we slept it was that our wives took the looks that showed what time and the grind were doing to us. And while we slept the house was quiet because our very young were put to bed and those of an age were out at play. And while we slept our ghosts slept in the well field: because our ghosts worked our day with us and were tired when we were tired.

We drank two pints of stout each working day: a pint at home before mid-day meal and a pint before bed with our own, in a pub that our own made their own of. Our bodies felt the need of those work-day pints. On the Saturday half-day we drank more than two because our minds it was that felt the need.

The need to talk long until we talked loud without knowing, to talk loud until we raised our voices further without knowing. Then we sang one by one until we sang together without knowing: and then we laughed without rightly knowing what all the laughter was about.

Our talk was about the past of our people when a craftsman was a man of substance with the past the present and the future of his children in his two craftsman's hands: it was then we talked long. We talked of our own day when a craftsman in his workshop spread the job of a day till it covered a week because the idle hand became a fist: it was then we talked loud. We talked of the new world of new people where the foot was forced to the shape of the boot, houses were poured with buckets into casings of board; where the house of prayer looked more a hall for song. It was then our voices climbed and travelled to the unheeding street.

Then someone would sing. Someone young would sing and the throat would be proud in the open neck of the Sunday shirt as the notes went from it loud and soft to rise and die, to ripple and leap, to laugh and sob and sigh and melt in quiet above our tilted faces. The singer was ours and the song was ours. The singer was theirs—the dead ones'. The song was theirs for the words had not changed. Nor had the singer changed. The face of his father and his father's father was under the tilt of the brown soft hat and the forelock heavy on the forehead. The power in the body, the blood in the veins, the heart crying in the voice were the power and the blood and the heart and the voice of his father's on through the listening years that were part of eternity now with the ghosts who walked when night put a careful corner of her shawl over the well field, and pinned it there with

30

four sharp, shining stars.

And it was in the pause between a song and a song that the two Leary brothers came the night we thought of giving them the well field.

There was the usual space between the coming of one brother and the other—a half dozen of the long one's long strides. Two days previous an uncle had died leaving only a childless wife and the two Leary brothers for his land and his riches. We never liked the uncle or the shrewd, stranger wife he was punished with. But we liked the two Leary brothers. When the short one stepped from the street we would have jibed at him about his chance of good fortune in the will, but for something about the way he walked to the counter. He was always quick on his feet and bold in display of his prominent belly: like the new Town Clerk when God gave him bad news about the old stock for the ears of the new Town Council. This time he was even quicker on his feet but less the big-drummer with his middle.

'Double whiskies,' he ordered.

'How are we, lads?' said the long one coming in.

There was something about him too. What he had in height was matched with weight well moulded onto big bones. He was smiling, but there was nothing new in that. His face under the tweed cap always hung in the part-sad, part-mocking smile of the born fighter who has been hit with all the other has and still is standing, and yet is powerless to get home with his own sledge-hammer blow. This time it was that the smile had a new shape: as if the other had hit him in a mean way and the smile was salted with a bleeding lip.

'Here's to the old stock anyhow,' he said and the glass only parted the smile as he drank.

'May they rest,' said the short one.

Suddenly a chuckle put sound to the long one's smile.

'I'm thinking what a hell of a hard time they're giving the uncle now,' he said.

And we knew straight away that the uncle had left them out of his will.

'How bad is it?' Jim Lannigan asked.

Jim was a woodcarver and the oldest of the old stock living.

'Couldn't be worse,' the short one answered.

'It could,' the long one disagreed. 'We could be dead with him and known to relatives for all eternity.'

'Nothing at all then?' Old Lannigan asked.

'Not even a mention,' said the short one.

'Not even to ask us for prayers for his soul,' said the long one. 'Because he knew he'd have them after the reading of the will.'

We had been certain of good fortune for them in the will. We all wished for it. Our women prayed for it. Our children knew it as the happy story waiting for an end. Our dead watched for it to make their heaven whole before they turned their faces smiling on eternity.

'Herself will have it all so,' Tom Breen, the oldest blacksmith said, his big hand gentle on his grey moustache.

'And she'll bring a stranger brood to fill the place of children,' growled Lyne, the painter.

'More new owners for old goods,' MacGillicuddy the stonecutter agreed, his dead left eye indifferent to the anger in the right.

'Changes for the better don't happen any more,' said Casey the stonemason.

It was not the uncle's money that mattered. It was not the houses or the car—or his power because that came from selling the soul of our kind for the new kind of soul. All we wanted for the two Leary brothers were the sandpit, the quarry and the two workshops. For here then would be two of the old stock who were men of substance still among the new people. Here would be a part of our town belonging where it properly belonged. Here would be two of our own who had it in their power to will a portion of our town to some of our own coming after: a stake to hold till maybe the new people would wear old and the old stock would come new into their own again. And then it was that someone said:

'What about the well field?'

There was a silence: in it the old and the young faces were as still as the pewter and bronze amid the gleam of the bottles. The sounds of the street grew big and drew near like a challenge. Sunlight through a high window lit up the nook where Old Lannigan sat, his grandson standing tall and young as his shoulder. The old man's hair and beard shone quiet like the pewter. The young one's red hair shone bold like the bronze. The dust in the sunlight softened the picture they made to tone like old masters. When Old Lannigan spoke the challenge of the street drew away again.

'The well field,' he said. 'What about the well field?'

'It belongs to the Learys,' said the son of the blacksmith.

'It belonged to them one time,' Old Lannigan corrected.

'It belongs to them still.'

'By right it do, but in law it don't.'

'Why so?' asked the son of the blacksmith.

'I'm no law man,' Old Lannigan said. 'But the way I heard of the law in this matter, the well field belongs to no one man or no one family any more.'

'The Learys never signed it over to any man,' the grandson of the stonemason argued.

'The law don't always look for a signature,' Old Lannigan explained. 'It seems that if a man laves a thing like a field open to public trespass for a number of years, that field becomes common property.'

'What is the number of years?' asked the grandson of a cooper.

Old Lannigan smiled.

'Far less than the years between us and the Learys who made that mistake,' he said.

'There's four generations of Learys between them and the two Leary brothers.'

'Time enough for a change in worlds,' said Tom Breen, the blacksmith.

'And for a change in Learys,' said the long Leary out of his new smile.

'Our kind don't change,' MacGillicuddy said quietly, his good eye as mild as the dead one.

'The world has changed,' the short Leary said. 'The only way we can have a place in life at all is
34

to bring a bit of our own world back.'

'We'll begin with the well field,' young Lannigan said.

'What can we do about the well field?' asked Old Lannigan, looking up at him.

'The town has a right to trespass on the well field—right?' asked the grandson.

Old Lannigan nodded agreement.

'Supposing the town gave up the right of trespass, wouldn't the field come back to the two Leary brothers?' the young Lannigan went on.

Old Lannigan thought for a moment, then shook his head.

'You'll never get them all to agree,' he said.

'If there isn't one way there's another,' said young Lannigan.

'Yes!' said the youngsters to a man.

'But is it fair to ask or to force?' Old Lannigan insisted.

'Aye,' the old ones gave agreement to the wisdom of the question.

But young Lannigan would not be shaken.

'What's not fair?' he said.

'Every scar on the crust of that field was made by our people before the new people ever came. The football part, the circus part, the tinkers' part along the wall, the courting pathway under the trees, the grass worn on the bank of the stream, the stone steps worn to the flag kneeler of the well itself: every single sign of life going and coming to that field is a sign made by our lives and the lives of no one else.'

'True!' agreed the young ones in a body.

Old Lannigan cupped his hands over the head of his stick. There was silence for a moment. Then his old voice dreamed away to agreement.

'And the dew on the trampled grass, and the webs that we break in the arch to take water from the well in the morning: they are put there while the ghosts of our kind walk the old ways when night is on the world.'

'Aye,' said the old man and the young together like an Amen to a prayer.

'We can try anyhow,' Old Lannigan said.

'We can start straight away,' young Lannigan said.

'We will start after last Mass to-morrow,' said Old Lannigan. 'When we have less of the drink in us and more of the grace of God.'

'After last Mass.'

Last Mass was our Mass on Sundays. At six o'clock, through the last of night and the first of day our women, cowled in shawls, went to Mass and Holy Communion. Mass and Holy Communion for our children at nine: but last Mass for our men always, except on Christmas mornings and Easter mornings when we went to Holy Communion too. To keep in the memory of our God, and ease the minds of our women and our priests.

Our God was a strong and a fair God. Our sins were made weak by the strength of their manner. Our church was worthy of our God.

The spire was so high that a twenty-foot cross at the top looked the size for a rosary. The dark oak ceilings were so far overhead that a lost bird lit by the eave windows looked as small and as bright as a moth near a candle. Candles on the altar looked remote from the porch as stars when they are nearest. The great organ broke like a storm of singing winds against the grey-blue granite of the walls. Yet even the high hidden inches that never would know the eye of man were a credit to the skill and care of our ghosts who built it.

Over the road from our church was our river. Over the river was our green-stone bridge, where the old stock met after last Mass for as long as our town was a town.

That Sunday in the shade of the alders by the bridge we began to talk again about the well field. The upshot of the talk was the final decision to ask each person of the new people to forgo their right of trespass on it. For thoroughness we agreed on a door to door talk with them, beginning with the business class.

Old Lannigan led the way, withered the way a tree withers, bent but with strength to the minute of the fall. Tom Breen the blacksmith on his left, the smooth clear skin of all blacksmiths clear and smooth still in spite of his years. On his right MacGillicuddy the stonecutter, like all stonecutters hewn into age as if Time in its turn used a mallet and chisel: his good eye watching Old Lannigan's stick so that his feet would not come in the way of it. All together in that town of new people we did not add to one hundred men. Age and near-aged at the front, youth in the middle and rear: the halter of years on old bones was a check on young tempers. The check was needed before all was said. The check did not hold before all was done.

Give them their due, the new business people agreed almost to a man. But in some cases the way they agreed left room for improvement. The well field meant nothing to them. Their lovers' walk led more imposing ways. Their children kicked football in a field that boasted regular goal-posts in place of the heap of little patched jackets. The circus of their day brought them richer and bigger wonders than cantering horses and tumbling clowns, so it called for more space than our field could give. Many of them hardly knew that our field was there at all. But some grew a new interest when we explained our errand. A new clutch tightened on the poor coin in the corner of the purse. Nevertheless, Old Lannigan's calm face or the blacksmith's great shoulders, or the quiet stare of the stonecutter's dead eye had their way. Where they had not, the flare of devil in younger eyes had. By nightfall we had accounted for the business portion of the new people.

Next evening after work we began on the new working class. Here we were taking our case to a harder court and we knew it. Many times on our rounds it took all the elders could do to hold young fists from flailing. We had never welcomed the new worker. It was not in our nature to say one thing and mean another, to hide a grudge with a show of smiles. Openly, honestly but none the less hurtfully we and our dead despised their jack-of-all-trades invasion of our world. One man one craft, was our motto; and the man for the craft must be bred to it. We shared the secrets of our craft with each other only. We refused to work with any but our own kind whose name in a craft was as old as the craft. As one man we walked away from an employer who took on any but men who were indentured to work with us. To get work the new worker had to cut wages and work a longer day. Their chances were poor enough, until the make-shift and the jerry-built became the order of the day. Then it was their turn to be up and our turn to be down. Their better fortune had not healed old wounds because day by day the handful that was left of us made the wounds to sting again. Nevertheless, we faced them, and they faced us. For our direct question they had a direct answer: a quiet No that for all its quietness bore a hint of challenge. Old Lannigan led us away to talk the matter over. Age at the front, youth in the middle and rear; and age was a good way gone before they discovered that youth had slipped back and away from the slow procession.

As Old Lannigan led the old ones towards the river bridge, the young Lannigan was leading the young ones into the new workers' district. The young ones of the new workers expected this and were advancing along the road to meet them. Not a voice was raised, no word was spoken as the two groups walked step for step towards a meeting on the quiet road. Only the trees could have seen, and beyond the trees the cross on the spire, beyond the cross the evening star: beyond the star the eyes of our dead looking back. From some faces colour drained, in others colour strengthened as the quiet road gave full value to the unhurried steps. No face showed a trace of the fear which panics where the shout is not there to dull the thud of the heart on the eardrum and words are not shared to steel the stiffened arm for the violence of the blow. No word, no shout, no tremor on the mask-set face. There never are where hate is seasoned through many years and blows are struck in the secret dream before life itself brings the time and the place. No sound on the quiet road, only march of men towards march of men, till man to man they met and fought with only the thud of the blow and the hiss of the breath to hear in the quietness that trees dusked with their shadows. The blows are hard that seasoned hate can strike. The blows are hard that seasoned hate can stand. Blood was the wine to quicken the spirit, hurt was the spur to hurt more. Quick, strong, vicious but always silent the young men fought in a moving wheeling tangled mass as Old Lannigan led the old ones back in search of the young.

'Stop!' he shouted on the fringe of the fight, but no one heeded.

'In God's name, stop!' he shouted again.

The bent back almost straightened as he raised his face like an angry old saint. But the fight went on. It was then that the long Leary, with a touch of the old smile on the shape of the new, spread his long arms and forced a way for Old Lannigan into the thick of the fighting so that he suffered no more than the loss of his hat.

'In the name of God, stop!' he shouted again, the stick raised high over his bare head.

'Stop, stop, stop!!!'

This time they heeded him. Their fury was bright in their eyes as they looked his way, so that for the instant it seemed as if their hate was for him.

'I'm ashamed of ye,' he said.

'When you were young yourself you did the same,' young Lannigan defended.

'And the old ones of my time did what I'm doing now,' said Old Lannigan. 'We were all of us in this from the start. It matters to all of us, whether young or old, and ye shouldn't have made a move that wasn't decided by all.'

'On our side the story is the same,' a voice as old as Lannigan's stated.

Even men of medium height hid the speaker from sight. When they stood aside a little bearded man with a skin as brown and wrinkled as an old leaf walked up to Old Lannigan and peered into his gun-dog face with a terrier's cheek. It was Timmie Hartigan, the oldest man among the new workers.

'It do seem,' said he, 'that the new and the old know the language of the fist.'

'The cunning of the craft don't rob the hand of force in a blow,' said Old Lannigan.

'It do seem,' said Old Hartigan, 'that ye were in earnest about the well field. Is there gold in it?'

'What's in it for us is not in it for ye,' said Old Lannigan.

'There's an answer for that, if I knew it,' said Hartigan.

'If you were born again,' said Old Lannigan.

'I wouldn't be born again if they made me the son of a king,' said Hartigan. 'Because there was bound to be trouble in my reign. But tell me, the answer ye got to that question ye put was deserved.'

'I don't follow,' Lannigan told him.

'The way the question is put calls the tune of the answer,' Hartigan explained. 'The way ye put the question ignored the fact that we had rights in that field. Ye didn't ask us, ye told us.'

'No one but a Leary has a right in life to the well field,' Old Lannigan stated.

'The world and its mother—may God forgive her —have a right in law,' said Hartigan.

'Do ye recognise that we have a share in that right? Do ye admit that it is right ye should ask us in a fair way for what it is our right to keep or to give? Do ye, now?'

'Are you talking in law or in life?' asked Old Lannigan.

'In law then,' said Hartigan.

'We're no law men,' Lannigan told him.

'We are when it suits us,' said Hartigan, jerking his quick little terrier head in impatience.

'So here then, do ye recognise our right in law to take the stand we took?'

'We have to,' said Old Lannigan. 'And here and now, we do.'

'Come home, lads, the battle is over,' said Hartigan, turning on his heel.

'One way or another it would end the same,' said Lannigan. 'Good evening to you.'

Then the two old men led their followers away, as dusk filled the lengthening space between them on the quiet road that the trees could see, and the cross on the spire, and beyond the cross the star. But beyond the star our dead no longer looked back. They had turned their faces smiling on eternity.

The high heads of the old ones were good to see.

The pain of the bruise was good to feel. The smile on the face of the long one was the smile of the game fighter who has been hit for almost the once too often, but at last has himself been able to hit. Steps were firm. Tongues were tied. Feeling was tight in the throat and hot at the back of the eyes. With fists clenched hard and teeth hard pressed together for control we walked high-headed past the new owners of that town that used to be ours.

Perhaps we knew it was the last time we all would walk together in that town. That could be. Because we knew where we came from we knew where we were going. Because we had had our day we knew the night was near. As night drew down about us we remembered the brightness of the morning and how strong the sun was on our faces when it struck upon our noon. Maybe we felt that when we walked together on the earth again there would be one the less with us, and one the more the length of a last breath away. Maybe we felt it in our bones that each new time we ever after walked together on the earth there would be one the less on the earth with us, and one the more walking the old ways when night spread that special corner of her shawl over the well field and pinned it there till dawn with four, sharp, shining stars. Lannigan. Breen. MacGillicuddy. Casey. One by one they left us. But leaving they left with us the well field for our daylight, and we left it for them when the daylight was gone.

We did proudly by the well field for them. Our blacksmiths gave it a gate. Our masons gave it a wall. Our carpenters gave it trellised fences to brace

43

the young spines of the cypress trees, which our gardeners borrowed from the new rich tenders of old gardens while their dogs were away. Our stone-cutters gave it new grey steps to the old stone kneeler by the well. Our woodcarvers gave it a story in seasoned oak for the niche above the arch of the well shelter.

And maybe we felt it was the last time we would have full freedom in our crafts in this new world of new methods. The iron gates were fit to stand between an eye and the moon: fine in the light as the art of the spider, all curl and scroll and flowering into shapes as graceful as blossom on drooped stem. And the story being forever told in mellow oak was about Joseph our patron saint, and Mary the nearest neighbour of our women, and Jesus whom our children knew well. Joseph stood at his carpenter's bench, Mary was in the doorway of the workshop holding an earthenware jar full to the brink with clear-cool water from the nearest well, Jesus with His child's hand was raising a cupful to the craftsman's hand of the carpenter.

As the years went by the cypresses grew into tall and dark green plumes. The field each year grew the shining golden mane of a meadow. With scythes we swept it gently from the root and let it lie, for the sun by day and the feet of our dead by night. When it was dry and the colour of pale light we drew it away and sold it to buy winter boots for our children. Shorn of the shining mane the crust of the field showed through the glinting stubble. And there they were again. The football pitch where we ran and rose and gripped and kicked, and argued

44

after as we panned the stream water with a plate of palms against our fire-hot faces. The circus ring, where mild-eyed horses, bits strapped to the breast-band on short leash to arch the columned necks, circled big and broad as if cast in bronze for bronze-cast horsemen, while little clowns with great noses and wide check trousers cart-wheeled for the laughter of our children. The tinkers' camping ground along the wall, where big-bosomed women combed long copper-coloured hair by faggot fires at night while their young fought sleep away with giddy laughter under the tilted spring-carts, and their men sang in drink together on the road home with ashplants beating time while ready to defend defenceless heads. The lovers' walk under the lime trees, where love grew that was blessed in the church of our God to last forever without end.

But each year fewer scythes were needed for fewer reapers, as more of our aged went on to our dead and more of our primed went on into age. And fewer pairs of boots were needed as our very young moved on into youth and went to care for themselves in other countries. The men of our kind were the first to pass on nearly always: and always their women followed in the next spring, if worry about a child or a grandchild did not hold them from going a while more. Men and women, they went on to our dead ones: the aged ones. The younger and young went over the seas, in search of a town where crafts were not forgotten and crafts-men not wholly neglected.

Each year there were faces missing among the gathering on the green-stone bridge after last Mass.

Until the year came when the shadow of the alders purpled the pipe-smoke of only the two Leary brothers. They held the field for our departed living and our dead departed and would not leave it. For five years there were only the two Leary brothers. Then in the spring of the sixth year the short Leary brother passed fussily away, and there was only the long one each Sunday on the bridge: elbows on the parapet, old smiling face between old gnarled craftsman's hands, smiling down on the amber river until the need to eat called him away. One Sunday he never left the bridge at all, or never stirred at all, but no one noticed because there was no one left to care whether he ate or not. No one noticed until a dog in the evening shivered on the leash and would not pass. The owner drew near the long one and looked into the old smiling face between old gnarled craftsman's hands, and knew that the eyes were not seeing the river. But he did not know, as we would have known, that the last had joined the rest to walk that night in the well field.

It was the last thing we owned in that town: the well field. But when we were all gone the new Town Clerk confided to the new Town Council that he knew all along that we never owned the well field at all, that it would have taken an Act of Parliament to give back to Learys what the law of trespass had taken from their ancestors, that anyhow it did not matter because the long Leary had willed the field to the old stock, and there were none of the old stock left, so even if the will were valid the field would belong to the Government of the country.

But he did not know, as we would have known, that the old stock walked together after nightfall in the well field. Further, the new Town Clerk suggested that the field, with its magnificent gate, shrined well and tall cypresses was ideal for what the new people had need of for a long time: A New Cemetery.

And so it came to pass that even our dead, to be together, must walk unfamiliar ways, or lie forever in unrest.

Dry Train

A cool breeze from the window made candlelight lap against the walls of the room as Miah opened his eyes. Minnie stooped over him with a candlestick in one old hand and an alarm clock in the other. Her ancient red dressing-gown was roped round her small body with a girdle like a monk's, her short grey pigtails stuck out behind her ears and with her eyes squinting into his face she had an oriental look about her.

'Time to stir, a quarter past five, you'll have a grand day for your trip, I can see by the stars in the window,' she said. 'Thanks be to God,' she put in like an afterthought as she moved out of the room in slippers as old as the dressing gown.

Starlight took over from candlelight at the window and the stillness made old Miah lie on for a while, trying to make sense of the train journey to Dublin ahead of him. No matter what way he looked at it he ended with the uncomfortable thought that a dry train, a rolling roaring pub with no beer, would be no place for a drinker of long standing and falling and always rising again.

'Tea is made,' Minnie called up from the foot of the stairs and he reached for his trousers. The smell of frying bacon met him on the top step to remind him of whiskey; most things in the morning reminded him of whiskey, especially frying bacon. 'Day train how are you,' he told himself ruefully, but the smile that was never far away from his face came back as he stepped into the kitchen. 'I'll wash before I eat,' he told Minnie and she switched on the light in the pantry. Minnie was nervous of electricity but she allowed it downstairs for light. He washed, combed his white hair and beard, and finished dressing to collar and tie and the last button in the waistcoat.

'Tea is poured,' Minnie called and he went to join her at the table. Beside his plate of bacon and eggs and a few curls of kidney were a mug of steaming tea and a glass of whiskey. 'God spare you, girl,' he said, raising the glass.

'That'll be your last before Dublin so I gave it extra,' Minnie said.

'How do you mean last, girl?' he asked between sipping the whiskey and licking of lips.

'You don't mean to tell me you're bringing drink on a Pioneer train?' she said.

'Who else would bring it, in God's name?' he answered, draining the glass.

'Don't bring God into this,' Minnie said with shock in her voice.

'Who made water into wine at the wedding feast?' Miah was quick to ask.

'He never made whiskey and you're going to no wedding,' Minnie was even quicker to answer.

Miah palmed a smile off his face to say: 'I filled the hip-flask to the brim at Jack C's last night. For the train like, in case of emergency like.'

After a long pause Minnie said: 'In case of emergency. I suppose 'tis all right. Like.'

'The journey is a kind of emergency in itself,' he reminded her. 'With priests and nuns in the company I fancy I'll be darted with questions like—"What's an old toper like you doing on a Pioneer pilgrimage?" Half in fun whole in earnest like.'

'Be serious,' Minnie said.

'Some of the other long-faces might think I was a spy in the camp.'

''Tis no pilgrimage. The Pioneer Total Abstinence Association is holding an All-Ireland rally in Dublin's Croke Park today.'

'How dare they,' Miah interjected. 'How dare they walk on sod made sacred by the footballers of this county for a century of All-Ireland finals.'

''Tis only for a day; we'll give it back to ye this evening,' Minnie said.

'Oh, thanks,' came from Miah in a way that made Minnie chuckle into her tea.

'Oh, I know you're having me on. 'Tis an old game of yours. I used to tell myself that laughing at me was better than being ignored,' she said, still chuckling.

'Who's laughing now? And who is she laughing

at?'

'Herself maybe,' said Minnie, wiping tears of one kind or another out of her eyes with the sleeve of her dressing-gown. 'But anyhow, you walk on that train as if you own it. Don't wear the cloak of a martyr with your tongue in your cheek. As a mason by trade, you can tame stone but sometimes you pretend you couldn't crack eggshells.'

'Oh here,' Miah protested but Minnie charged on. 'I'm the Pioneer and 'tis I bought the tickets. We weren't going to the rally, we were going to spend the day with our son Shay and his wife Kitty and their small sons, our grandsons, Mark and Danny. My sister Ellie was taken to hospital last night gasping for breath with bronchitis. So I have to stand by Ellie and you have to brave the dry train on your own. And if anyone, anyone, I say, if anyone says you have to be teetotal to travel on that train I'll deal with them personally, you tell them that.'

After a pause to draw breath she added: 'Now put on your hat, 'tis a quarter to six and 'tis Sunday, so you have to go to Mass in the friary on your way to the station.'

Miah finished his tea and got ready for the road while Minnie fussed about preparing for the send-off. 'Now,' she said, facing him on the porch, 'let me look at you.' She took his hat off and put it back on again to her liking. She tucked a well pressed white handkerchief into the breast pocket of his jacket and put another into a side pocket.

'Have you your ticket?' she asked.

'Yes,' said Miah.

'Have you your pipe and tobacco?'

'Yes.'

'Have you your specs and the book you're reading?'

'Yes.'

'Is the paper money safe in your waistcoat pocket?'

'Yes.'

'And have you the flask for emergency?'

'On my hip,' said Miah as he opened the door.

The rag-doll shape with the stick-out pigtails was waving to him from the lighted porch as he closed the garden gate behind him. He raised his hand in answer before he stepped out of her sight.

The footsteps echoed across the street in the still starry dark until the silence was shattered by the tolling of the friary bell. When the silence settled back after the last toll a blackbird was singing in the friary orchard. Light in colours shone through the stained glass windows of the chapel but by now there was just enough daylight to see the steps. They were littered with bagpipes and side-drums and kettle drums.

A big drum was where a banner hung from a crested pole in the porch; the town's pipe band was travelling with the teetotallers. As he treaded carefully past the instruments he couldn't help but think that as much whiskey and beer as spittle had dribbled though the pipes down the years. He would have laughed if he wasn't sidling past the big drum and the banner in to Mass.

He left the chapel a few minutes before Mass was over to find that daylight had won the battle with the stars. When he had negotiated the many steps down from the chapel hill he was only the width of a road and the length of an avenue away from the railway station. He was stepping into an empty carriage in the long train when he heard the pipes playing the remainder of the congregation up the avenue. By the time pipers and pilgrims were boarding the train Miah had his own pipe going and his cowboy book ready to hide in if his carriage was invaded by Pioneers.

He felt lucky when no one came near him until the train was on the move, and then it was a six-foot youngster who tugged the carriage door open, leaped aboard with a soft leather grip in his fist and said 'Morning, sir,' with an American accent. A sunburst hit the tanned face and fair hair of the Yank as the train left the station. He put the grip on the seat opposite Miah and sat beside it.

'Morning, boy,' said Miah.

'I'm a soldier on short leave from Sam's Army in Berlin,' the Yank said.

'You have the cut of an officer,' Miah told him.

'Rookie second lootenant pilot on his last chance to toe the line,' said the Yank. 'As it is, I'm overdue at the base so I took advantage of the Sunday train to make time and grab a sleep.'

'You're in the right place for that,' Miah encouraged with the smile that people who didn't know him called saintly. 'I'm a stone mason and I'm the quietest man on earth when I haven't a hammer and chisel in my hands.'

'With that white beard and hair you look patriarchal,' the Yank told him.

'Moses without the stones,' said Miah and the Yank grinned and said 'Yeah!' in approval.

'Look, sir,' said the Yank, 'last night I had one hell of a time at a good-bye party, so I'll grab a nap now if you'll excuse me.'

'I'll be the look-out,' said Miah, leaning forward in mock seriousness.

'Yeah,' said the Yank with a conspiratorial finger to his lips. He stretched full length on the long seat with the soft grip for a pillow. 'Yeah,' he said again before sleep came with the closing of his eyes.

Miah admired the way the mountains were taking the sun before the train swept him into lower ground where fields and trees and streams seemed nearer in the finger-flick glimpses that speed allowed. On the roads around wayside villages people were walking or cycling or driving to Mass; mostly driving.

He read through the rest of the way to Mallow where the train took on three more bands and hundreds of Pioneers. Any of the newcomers who approached the carriage went elsewhere on seeing that the long Yank occupied half of the seating space. That suited Miah down to the ground.

He read and smoked all the way to the stop at Limerick Junction, where again it was a case of more bands, more Pioneers and still more sleep for the Yank. Bare-headed women with white aprons sold fruit out of baskets from carriage to carriage along the platform. Miah bought six oranges in a brown paper bag for his grandchildren and the dealer told him he looked like St. Francis as she gave him his change. 'Here's my blessing,' he told
54

her, raising his hand as the train moved away, and she was waving and laughing in the last that he saw of her.

'Where am I?' The Yank was speaking with one eye open as the train beat out a top speed tattoo on the rails.

'You're not a long way from Tipperary now, soldier. You're in it,' Miah told him.

The Yank swung upright, combing his hair with his fingers. 'Cow country,' he said looking through the window. 'Hey, you're a Wild West fan like myself,' he added, pointing to the bucking broncho on the cover of Miah's paperback.

'Heading into Arizona in this chapter,' Miah told him and the Yank said 'Thirst country.' He added: 'Hey, which way is the bar on this train?' Miah said, 'No way,' and the Yank shot to his feet. 'Jesus,' he said, and it was no prayer.

Miah broke the news about the dry train but he cushioned the shock by taking the flask off his hip. 'My wife said to keep this for an emergency and this is an emergency surely,' he said. 'Take it and you'll feel better.' The Yank unscrewed the top of the flask and with a toss of his head drank half of what was in it. 'Fit for the gods, pardner' he said. 'Now you drink the rest to seal the pardner-ship.' Miah drained the flask and said 'Holy Water.'

'Now we'll break camp, pardner,' the Yank told him. 'You grab that cowboy book and your parcel and we'll hit the trail down these corridors.' He snatched his grip off the seat as he headed out of the carriage. 'Give your horse his head and stay on my tail. Yippee!'

The train was rocking and roaring with speed as they passed carriage after carriage with landscapes flicking by in the windows. 'Bumpy ride, pardner, like a stage coach. Stay in the saddle,' the Yank said as they swayed through a dining carriage that smelled of fried bacon where Pioneers were attacking rashers and eggs with knives and forks.

'End of trail will be in the guard's van' said the Yank, and they passed five carriages more before he said: 'Here it is.'

He paused at the van door to take a crisp five dollar bill out of a leather wallet. 'We'd better hope that the guard is a nice guy,' he told Miah.

'I'm praying,' said Miah with a face to match.

'Here goes,' said the Yank. Then he stepped ahead drawling: 'Hope we're not disturbing you, sir, but would you have the change of this?' He dropped the grip on the bare boards of the van floor and had the note between the guard's palms before he knew it.

'I'm afraid not,' the guard answered. He was sitting on one of four empty crates on the van floor.

'Keep it, I don't want it,' the Yank said.

The guard shot to his feet to get his bearings, but the way he made the note disappear into his waistcoat pocket would have done credit to a conjurer. He looked as young as the Yank as he sized up his visitors, but before he could get a word out the Yank was saying: 'Stand easy, guard, we come in peace for a pow-wow.'

'And for a pow-wow we need firewater,' he added as he sat on a vacant crate, put his grip on another between him and the guard, opened the
56

grip with a flourish, and there on top of crumpled pyjamas and shirts were two bottles of whiskey.

The guard's dark eyes showed their whites in delight, a grin spread slowly across his face as he subsided onto his crate: ''Twas God that sent ye,' he said in the sing-song accent of a Corkman. Miah smiled, preened his moustache with his fingers and pulled the fourth crate under him without a word.

As the Yank broke the seal on one of the bottles he explained: 'I was sick-sober when I got on this train without knowing it was dry. When he thought I was going to jump out the window this kind stranger snatched a flask off his hip in the fastest draw since Billy the Kid, and I murdered it. Now the stranger and I are pardners and I want to share a bottle with him to make up for the sudden death of his flask.' He raised the bottle to the light in the barred window of the carriage and added: 'And we want you to join us in the sealing of the partnership.'

The guard reached into the corner behind him and put three cups one after the other on the make-shift table. He tossed the spoon that was in one of them over his shoulder and said: 'One thing I hate about cups for whiskey is that you can't see the colour of the liquor, and that's a shame.'

'Cups that leaked would be worse,' said the Yank as he poured for the three of them. 'Here's to temperance,' he added, raising his cup. 'To temperance,' echoed the other two, lifting their cups above their noses. The three heads leaned backward to drink and bowed forward between swallows like a ritual. The ritual kept going as the Yank kept pouring and no one said a word.

Then the guard took time out to admire the seasoned way Miah was relishing the liquor. He tilted his peaked cap back to let a lick of black hair spring loose on his forehead. 'How in God's name did a man like you stray onto a dry train?' he asked Miah, his round face wearing the ghost of a grin that is the seal of contentment.

'My son, only son, only child,' said Miah. 'He's a teacher in Dublin with a lovely girl for a wife and two small sons, my grandsons, Mark and Danny. Put in my wife Minnie and that's all there is of us. I know the kids because they come down to us for holidays, but I'm coming to see them for a day and this is the only train travelling. The return half of my ticket is in my pocket.'

'They'll say you're a spy in the camp. They'll say the three of us are spies,' said the guard, nodding his head in agreement with himself.

By this time a spotlight of sunshine slanted through the window on the three men, making the buttons on the guard's black uniform look like real silver. Miah had taken off his hat and his hair looked like platinum. The Yank was in red pullover and blue slacks, and the tartan check in his shirt looked as loud as a fairground barker. Though still at top speed the train seemed more settled in itself. There was calypso rhythm in the sounds it made. It lulled the three into a silence of thinking and drinking not caring a damn as they sped through the miles.

All of a sudden the Yank said: 'Let's drink to Mark and Danny, the two very young colts in my pardner's far paddock. May they ride easy on all

58

their trails.' And the three touched cups, looked upward, swallowed and bowed together again for a refill.

'What do you mean paddock?' asked the guard.

'Surely you must have read cowboy books, like me and my pardner. My old man at home had shelves of them. Books by Zane Grey,' said the Yank.

'Lone Star Ranger,' said Miah.

'Charles E. Mulford,' said the Yank.

'The Bar-Twenty,' said Miah.

'Buck Peters,' prompted the Yank.

'Johnny Nelson and Hopalong Cassidy,' said Miah.

And Miah kept on cue until the Yank had to laugh with delight at the way the guard was gaping at the verbal give and take.

'Old cowboys, old trails,' said the Yank.

'Men like Hoppy,' said Miah.

'They got saddle soreness so often they ended up with leather asses,' the Yank said.

'Leather asses,' echoed the guard, choking with chuckles.

'That's one of two reasons why you never heard of their being shot in the ass; the arrows and bullets hopped off. The other is that they never ran away,' the Yank told him.

'Good men,' said Miah, downing a drink.

'Good guns,' said the Yank, pouring another. 'The Winchester. The old Colt forty-fives worn on the hip by ordinary mortals, but slung low on the thigh by the gods of the lightning draw. Yippee!!'

Miah smiled for the second time that day at
59

something like the war-cry of a Comanche being converted into the yelp of a cowhand on a spree. But the guard said: 'That was a bit on the loud side, partner. We mustn't forget that we're travelling with Pioneers.'

'Pioneers,' said the Yank. 'The men and women of the old West were the real pioneers. This is a diesel, theirs was a wagon train. And the Irish were up front in that kind of pioneering; opening up God's country between raid after raid by the Crow and the Cree and the Sioux and the Iriquois.'

'Here's to pioneers who drank firewater before breakfast,' said Miah.

'To pioneers,' said the others, and all three drank as one man.

Suddenly the Yank said: 'Hey, we're beginning to get into our cups.'

'We'll have to get out of them again in a hurry,' said the guard. 'We're not in the Wild West now. We're heading out of Kildare at a fair clip and 'tis Dublin City not Dodge City that's round the next few loops in the line.'

He got to his feet and put the empty cups back in the corner with the spoon. 'Tidy up, lads, leave no clues,' he said. The Yank closed his grip and gave what was left of the second bottle to the guard. 'You'll know what to do with that later.' The guard winked agreement and slid the bottle into the lining pocket in an overcoat that hung from a nail over the cups. 'I'll back-trail to check on the dry train pioneers,' he said, putting a finger to his lips to signal caution as he left the van.

The Yank joined Miah at the window. 'We've

passed the last wayside station,' Miah told him.

'I'll have to dash for a taxi to the airport the moment the train stops,' said the Yank. 'I'll have no time to say anything except so-long. As a last favour I want you to give these to young Mark and Danny.' He handed two crisp dollar bills to Miah. "I'd make it more but for the fact that if they're taken after their grandad they might go out and get drunk on a Pioneer train."

"Ye're dead lucky,' said the guard from the doorway. 'The nearest carriage to us is empty, so grab ye'r gear and get into it now. From there ye can leave with the rest of the passengers and no one will notice that ye've been here in the van. Now good luck, ye were the best of company.'

Miah persuaded himself that it was the train and not the whiskey that made him a bit unsteady on the way to the empty carriage with the oranges, but he was glad to be on a soft seat again. It seemed only a few minutes until the slowing train shuddered to a halt. 'I'm away,' said the Yank. 'No yippees,' said Miah. 'No reason,' said the Yank as he leaped onto the platform and raced away with the grip held high over his head.

For Miah it seemed a very deep step from carriage to platform. He stumbled without falling but the bag with the oranges dropped and burst on the ground. Four of the oranges rolled under the train; the other two rolled together away from him. He hurried after them, picked them up when they stopped, polished them with a cuff of his jacket and put one in each of his side pockets. He was so vexed at the thought of how foolish he must have

61

looked that it was a relief to see that the hundreds who hurried by hadn't the time to take notice.

He steered a wavering course through the Pioneers to the Liffey wall at the far side of the platform. By that time the crowd was leaving by the station gates or crossing the bridge over the river. And it was then that his grandsons came bounding towards him with shouts of 'Grandad, Grandad!' His son Shay was on their heels. Miah had barely time to touch his son's outstretched hand before the children grabbed him. One was as dark as the other was fair and both were pulling at him as if they wanted to make sure he was real. When he took the oranges out of his pockets they stopped.

'Oranges all the way from Grandma,' he told them.

'Why didn't she come?' asked Shay.

'Your Aunt Ellie isn't well and your Mam stayed to keep an eye on her,' Miah explained. 'Now, ye two young critters stand there before me and close ye'r eyes so tight ye'r noses will crinkle.'

Knowing that the words always came before a gift of some kind, Mark and Danny did as they were told. Shay grinned as Miah took the folded dollars out of his waistcoat pocket, rubbed them flat between his palms and with one in each hand raised them above the two young faces.

'Now open your eyes,' said Miah. Their big eyes got bigger at sight of the new notes. 'A real tall cowboy from Texas that I met on the train gave me these dollars for ye,' he told them. 'He said ye were to ride into town and paint it red and say "Yippee!" '

'Now say "Yippee" ' he told them as he put the notes into their hands with a flourish. 'Yippee,' they yelled and they went on yelling 'Yippee' as they ran side by side towards the gates and the bridge with the notes held high over their heads.

Shay was grinning as he fell into step with his father to follow them. But Miah's smile looked fit for a halo.

The More We Are Together

1

The brothers were the last two coopers left in that town.

Other crafts were going: theirs was gone. Now they got a few pocket-warm shillings from farmers for repairing things they had made years ago. Mick, with a head full of reading at his beck (Shakespeare, Service and the Bible were all the one as long as they came under candle light without cost) was apt to dramatise their position. Charlie would tell him to have a bit of sense, if he would spare the words. The two lived together in the narrowest lane in that town, in a house so small that even under-sized Mick looked big in it and Charlie looked like a heron in a hencoop.

Charlie looked like a heron anywhere. Long and

lean and droop-nosed, eye-weary with boredom even in a pub, when he stood he drew one leg up till the flat of a thin sole against wall, bar or lamp-post braced the cushion of the calf for the right buttock: then his stubbled craw collapsed into a loop of neck band, hands dug into trouser pockets, elbows hugged the shelter of his withers, a Wood-bine hung limp from his sad mouth like a sprat from the beak of the bird he resembled. He spoke when he had to speak, but mostly he used a high sweet whistle of a tune for ironic comment on things about him. Although he grudged life every step he gave to it he would walk any distance in the funeral of a man he liked. He was never known to walk in the funeral of a woman.

Mick was partial to women, but his square chunk of body on short legs and the music-hall humour of his face never prompted their love sense to sacrifice, and hard times to his trade estranged their sense of good business. In the wind-up he drew consolation from their nearness passing in the narrow lane. His small blue-bright eyes signalled his moods as far in daylight as a cat's eyes show at night. They told if he was liquored and ready for a spate on the passing away of the old stock, probing for doubtful beginnings to a new townsman or romancing about all the comely women who had loved and lost him up the laneway to Charlie.

The under half of the house was their workshop, its floor a good twelve inches above the cobbled lane level with whole generations of coopers' chips and shavings. In a deep poke of window in the back wall was a statue of Our Lady and a corkscrew. Over the workshop was the loft, where they slept on two beds in two whorls of old clothes. A ladder led to the loft and it was when Charlie was one night climbing the ladder that Mick first noticed he was having trouble with his left leg.

'What's up with you?' Mick asked.

'My leg,' Charlie gave back on two darts of a Woodbine.

'I know 'tis your leg, man,' said Mick.

'Then you know as much as I do,' said Charlie.

Lying on the doss that night Mick lighted a second pipeful of twist. The smoke plumed up out of murk to full whiteness in a splinter of moonlight from a chink in the slates. Charlie's head lay in the light, his face becalmed in sleep. The candle, stuck with its own grease to the bed above Mick's head, was not lighted that night for reading.

2

Down in the workshop in the morning, boiling a can of water in the oil stove, Mick talked up through the hole where the ladder reached the loft.

'Charleen! Charleen, I said!'

'I can't hear you,' said Charlie, half out of sleep.

'Why so, man?'

'I don't want to.'

'Why so, man?'

'Guess away.'

'Charleen! Charleen, I said!'

'Well?'

'What about the leg, Charleen?'

'What about the cup of tay?'

'Will you see a doctor?'

'In hell with the rest.'

'If I was you I would, man,' Mick ventured.

'You're not me,' said Charlie.

Mick jambed his hat down to an inch above his eyebrows. He allowed a pause, then tried again.

'Charleen!!'

'Go to hell.'

'About the leg.'

'That's what I mean.'

'I was looking at you last night . . . You were asleep. There was moonlight through the hole above my left ear slantin'. . . . You were pinned by the light like St. Paul near Damascus. . . . You made such a spittin' image of a corpse that I smoked half the night over it. . . . Maybe if you don't see a doctor we'll play the piece out in rale earnest—will you see a doctor?'

'No,' Charlie grunted at last.

'Then I'm as well layin' in the tobaccy and drink?'

'You're as well.'

'Then come down and wet your own bloody tay!' Mick shouted up through the hole.

But he thought of opening the door in time to see the women from Mass.

3

The leg got worse. Charlie's heron-perch against uprights became as much necessity as the habit of years. Climbing the ladder was as difficult sober as ever it had been in drink. Mick heckled him from all angles without success. In time the night came when Charlie could not climb the ladder at all. He tried drawing himself up the stilts of the ladder with his arms. He failed because the old strength had all but left him. He crouched to sit on the third rung, lit a Woodbine and looked up to find Mick's shadow between him and the doorway of starlight. With the slightly swaying shadow had come the smell of drink. There was derision in the croon of Mick's voice when he spoke.

'Home is the sailor, home from the sea,' he quoted. 'Home for good an' all,' he added, circling a finger in the air towards Charlie.

'When the sailor can't climb the riggin' his sailin' days are done. He didn't make off the ould medicine chest in time. Or throw the bottle overboard in time. So now the stars will sail without him ... and gulls will bring their cards to him a mile inshore.'

Charlie's strong tugs at the fag put little haloes of warm light about his head that found his face unmoved.

''Tis a grand night for a man with two legs,' he said.

Mick rocked, toppled and went out of sight to the shavings.

'If he could stand on 'em,' Charlie added.

From where Mick lay came a stirring of shavings, the jerk of a breath as he heaved himself to sitting, then the voice crooning: 'Joke away, Charleen, split the ould sides with choked laughin' at boozed Mick but remember.... Remember, Charleen, remember, my man, that Mick will be game ball in the mornin' ...'

In a high sweet whistle Charlie began 'After The Ball Was Over'. Mick shook himself for the rattle of his matches. He lighted a match to find the pocket with his pipe. The match dropped from his hand and lit an oak chip. The chip flared and passed the flame to chips near it, all seasoned with years of shelter. In a minute there was a small steady blaze and the sweet smell of mellow wood burning. Hat askew, Mick gaped at the firm growing blaze. Of a sudden his eyes widened and brightened in the rising light with a wild, unuttered laughter. The quick jog of a thought enlivened the body. He tensed inside his loose hand-me-down clothes and rose to his feet to teeter about the workshop, grabbing and groping for bits and pieces of solid timber, piling them on the strengthening blaze from the floor. He began to shout wide-mouthed, snapping at the words with his stained teeth.

'I know now what we'll do, Captain. We'll burn the ould ship in dry dock, Captain, and go from sight and sound in a blaze of glory. No creepin' to death and crawlin' to graves for the last of the coopers. O Merciful God, that thought of this for us! O Merciful God, to save our face! We'll go out on our legs! Out on our legs we'll go, Charleen, and the stranger round us dazzled by the blaze! Charleen, Captain, stand up and give me a hand with the glory, lend me a hand for the blazin' way home!! Charleen!!'

Charlie never stirred. He lit a second smoke from the end of the first. By this time Mick's shadow was large on the wall, dancing with Mick who danced with the flames, his voice kindling with the rising heat into round after round of mad merriment, louder and stronger. In the middle of it all he thought of the oil stove. He unscrewed the cap of the oil container and flung paraffin to burst above the blaze into sickles of hissing flame.

'Climb!' he shouted. 'Climb to the roof, ye sweet bitches of flame. Climb! Burn! Burn and roast us out of here forever more! Charleen, come and stand with me, opposite them out we'll stand together and laugh! They thought they were great coming to take our town away from us and our living away from us and our *women* away from us! Charleen, come here and cock your game leg in their foolish bloody stranger faces—and we'll laugh! Laugh, Charleen!'

The flames were licking the boards of the loft when the first of the townspeople arrived with buckets of water from the lane pump. Mick raved and cursed and got in their way till they lifted him kicking out of the place. Out in the lane his ravings followed the bucket chain from pump to house and back again, over and over. They grew in abandon as the fire was gapped with water and thick shrouds of smoke wound about each dancing shape of flame. When the last flame fell under weight of water he stopped shouting. He went limp as if the fire had been a part of the demon in him. The small house hissed in its walls like a shower on sheet water and belched great clouds of smelling smoke through the doorway.

Suddenly Mick's body shuddered. It straightened itself quietly and slowly as with a long-drawn breath. Then suddenly his wide mouth opened full out and

70

sharp as a dog's bark he cried—'Charleen!' He began to run towards the house thudding people right and left off his road and shouting—'Charleen!' But as he got to the house the heron-spare length of Charlie brought the game leg leisurely through the doorway. His clothes were sodden with flung water. His face and hands were as black as a sweep's. Mick blundered up, gripped his shoulders and shouted to his face as if it were up among the stars: 'Are you all right, Charleen? Are you all right, boy?'

'The least you might have done was to wet the cup of tay,' said Charlie.

4

They spent the night sitting by the hearth of the only old stock neighbour left to them: Mick drained of strength and sore for liquor, Charlie's sick bones craving heat through wet clothes from a fading fire. Charlie was still smoking when Mick nodded off in the small hours.

When Mick woke the first splink of cold dawn at the window showed him Charlie's long-drawn body limp in sleep over the chair. He had to fight an urge to listen for his brother's breathing. Sense arrived in time to remind him what Charlie would put into a few words if he opened an eye and found him fussing. Then memory had the firing antic ready for him: when he blasphemed a thick tongue disturbed the coat of wryness in his mouth. He went to grope for milk in the stale-smelling cupboard. He found enough to cool his mouth and leave a drop for the breakfast crust. Then he moved towards the door and tripped over a potato sack on the floor. He thought of a use for the sack: it would keep the dawn cold from Charlie's sick leg. He had the sack raised over the leg when a doubt about the depth of Charlie's sleep again unnerved him. Charlie could put a lot into a few words. A fire in the hearth would do, he thought. A timber catbox of straw against the hob would kindle and spit sparks at a touch of a match. But Charlie would remember the last match he struck. Charlie might open an eye. Charlie could put a lot into a few words.

He stood over Charlie's face, grey and drawn in the white weak light, and glared down at it.

'If you die of the cold you can blame your own bloody self,' he hissed.

Then he went and raised the latch with care and let himself onto the narrow lane.

Going to the small house now was like easing his way back to a near one he had offended during a skite on whiskey: like nearing the mother's presence knowing he had broken the last of her marriage tea cups in a drunken tantrum. There was the silence, the meeting side-face, the waiting of each for a sign from the other that it was all in a life and could go to the dead day that brought it. But unlike the old mother the small house gave no sign. He felt that maybe it was whatever of the mother was left in the house that gave no sign. He told himself to hell with that too. Still he stood there between the night and day in the narrow place, looking lost, until full daylight sent the dregs of night away and the presence lifted from inside the walls.

72

Then he chucked at the hat for courage and hummed his way into what was left of the workshop.

The carpet of chips and shavings had a great black hole in it. The steel of the tools lay in the hole, where bench and boxes and handles had left them in the fire. Metal hoops lay where the old barrel or firkin had been, or the tubs that farmers' wives had used to wash for the family or stall-feed a beast. Against one wall a hole was burned in the loft and a leg of Mick's bed stuck through. The ladder and Charlie had been farthest from the flames: the ladder still was there, leading to the loft. As he surveyed the damage a thought about the loft came to Mick. It sent him searching till he located a handsaw. He gave a grunt of satisfaction that enough of the handle was there to grip it.

He took off his jacket and hung it on the door latch. First he cleared the litter from the floor onto the lane cobbles. Then he journeyed up and down the ladder until he had rid the loft of all on it, from the pair of beds to the ha'penny candle. That done he returned into the workshop with the saw.

Three spars of timber, embedded in the stone of the side walls, supported the loft. Because a board was missing on either side the spars were clear for sawing where they met the walls. Standing on the ladder he sawed the centre spar free. Next he sawed the spar-shanks in the opposite blind angles. The loft still held above his head. Then he tackled the shank in the angle opposite the open door. Here he had to be careful that the ladder braced the corner of the loft when the saw had cut through. He backed slowly towards the doorway, easing the ladder with its burden down the wall. The loft now listed above him. Only the corner near the door held a grip on the house. Bracing it in turn with the ladder he sawed it free. Then he stepped on to the lane and jerked the ladder through the doorway after him. The loft fell to the ground, and there and then was a floor of boards.

Straight away he reassembled the beds in the workshop and put the litter from the lane into order inside. That done he sat on his bed to wait for Charlie. But the day aged without Charlie's coming. Mick went and dogged the sunlight through hour after hour, from street to street, gable to gable: knowing Charlie's custom in an idle day. When the sun had set he searched the pubs: without result. Night came down in a drizzle of mist. Globules of the mist on the leaf of Mick's hat glistened in the lane gaslight as he returned to the shelter of the house.

He was in an hour before Charlie limped up the narrow way, the long body crow-black against the silver the gaslight made out of wet cobbles. When he stooped in at the doorway the quiet light of the ha'penny dip was all the welcome he got. Mick was stretched on his bed, the hat on his face, his bald crown airing. Charlie abandoned his exhaustion to the bed opposite and lit another fag. There was a long silence before Mick raised the hat off his mouth.

'Well?' he challenged.

'Well?' Charlie gave back.

'What the hell were you doin' all day?'

'Makin' up my mind to see a doctor,' said Charlie.

'And where were you all night?'

'Seein' wan.'

Mick lay quiet for a while. Then he tilted the hat off the near eye and fixed Charlie with a glare.

'What the hell did he say, man, what did he say, tell us that much!'

Charlie took his time. Mick's barrel chest filled with a long breath.

'That I'll not do a long journey on two legs, but I might go a bit farther on one,' said Charlie.

Mick let the breath out easy. He let the hat fall back on his face. There was another silence before he spoke from under it.

'Well, wan leg is better than no leg at all,' he said.

'I'd rather the short journey,' said Charlie.

'What do you mane?'

'When I lave I'll lave all in wan piece.'

'You must have it in your mind to lave early,' said Mick.

'All in wan piece,' Charlie repeated amicably.

Suddenly Mick jerked to a tailor squat on the heap of old clothes. The hat fell in his lap. Tufts of hair stood out over his temples. The whites of his eyes looked genuinely clean against dark stubble and the prickles of a black moustache. The eyes glared at Charlie.

'Why all in wan piece, tell me?'

''Tis what any wan of them would have done.'

'Who's them?'

'Your old stock.'

'Through bloody ignorance,' said Mick. 'I know the story backwards. Better die of what ails you than own it and admit it as a weakness in the blood.

Ignorance, I say.'

'We're ignorant people,' said Charlie.

'Not all of us,' said Mick.

Charlie stretched his hand to make an arc of smoke with the Woodbine that for an instant linked the two beds.

'The half of what's left of us is,' he said.

'I won't argue with you,' said Mick. 'I'll spare my breath to blow froth, or whistle for a woman in a lonesome night.'

As another silence settled Charlie pierced it with a thin ironic whistle of a lovely air. The irony was in the beauty of his rendering. The tune was 'She moved through the fair' and Mick was caught in the imagery of its words: the young girl went from him through the country fair and away along a lakeside homeward under one star—until the irony went home to him and he hit back like a goaded animal.

'You're as ignorant as all the obstinate ould codgers that went before us,' he said.

'What do their ignorance matter to them now?' asked Charlie.

'It don't matter to them,' said Mick, 'but it do matter to us. They left us a legacy in a way of life it would puzzle a hermit to follow. Nothin' would do 'em but principle. They must have slept it, ate it and used it for firin'. Honesty was the best policy. A good day's work for a beggar's pay an' the rest was in the hands of the Good God Above. What did principle give 'em?'

'They could meet themselves in the mornin' shavin'' Charlie answered.

'What did honesty give 'em?'

'Sleep of a night.'

'And from the hands of the Good God Above?'

'The five of trumps in the last card dealt.'

'Aye, but sometimes you'd wonder if there's damn all in the "kitty",' growled Mick.

He rose, hat in hand, to pace the boards between the two beds. Suddenly he wheeled on Charlie.

'What I can't understand is why you feel you owe it to them to die sooner than you can help,' he said.

'What do extra time mean in the wind-up?' asked Charlie.

Mick gave the answer in a breath.

'A few times more to blow froth. A few times more to covet a young girl well made under the gloss of her white pelt. A few times more to tell the stranger to his face that he's no good.'

'A few times more to hold forth in praise of the old stock,' Charlie reminded.

'Oh, may God forgive me,' Mick prayed.

'As two of 'em we lived,' Charlie reminded.

''Tis time for a change,' Mick argued.

'Change before death,' smiled Charlie.

Mick jambed the hat on his head and flung open the door. The rain was falling fast and heavy now. It pounded the cobbles so that their silver leaped like a meshful of moonlit fish.

'O God, is it any wonder that sooner and later the sky has a leak on all the bloody world!' he called aloud into the lane.

5

The burning of the house brought problems they had not bargained for. Neither house nor workshop was insured. Property not theirs was burned and the code of their kind took for granted that the owners should be compensated. More customers were needed with tubs and firkins to mend.

They prepared by whittling handles for the damaged tools and edging the steel on whetstones wetted with spittle. The beds with their tatters were rolled against the back wall and hidden from callers with patchwork of old sacking on thick twine. In the new sleeping place the statue of Our Lady, coomed with untroubled dust as soft as moth wings, came into its own in time of candle light.

No further clients came their way. For four days the two appeared and disappeared through the parting in the canvas curtains, like two actors of the fit-up stage impatient for the arrival of an audience: Mick, a blubber-faced comic in trouble with remembering his lines; Charlie, the tragedian rehearsing a limp and limbering a selection from his store of smiles. After that much waiting the comic downed tools.

'Charleen.'

'Well?'

'For all we'd know, stayin' here, the world might be dead.'

'Or we might be dead to the world,' said Charlie.

'Well either we or the world must find out, an'

I see no sign of the world flockin' to the door,'
Mick said. 'There's only three days to market day
an' then the rustics will be in to moan over their
few relics like they were gold. Be the holy, talkin'
to their big fed bodies with their warm fat purses
I feel like a corpse with the pennies on my lids.
What'll we do at all?'

Charlie's answer was a whistle. The tune had run
its course before Mick recognised it as a comment,
and only then because in his mind the air was
wedded to its words:—

> 'The more we are together, together, together,
> The more we are together the merrier we will be:
> For your friends are my friends
> And my friends are your friends,
> So the more we are together the merrier we
> will be.'

Mick flung his hat on the floor and kicked it.

'Put a string on the whistle,' he said. 'What'll we
do about the long faces from the fields?'

'There's three days before us,' said Charlie.

'An' three centuries behind us that ended with
the fire,' said Mick in a breath. ''Tis no use. Ah,
can't you see 'tis no use. When the smell of the
craft went out of the house the craft went with it
and all the soul of the craftsmen, damned or
saved, sad or merry. All they thought and felt
and fought for, all they lived and hoped for, all
the sport they ever had and all the memories of
all they did at work or in drink: 'tis all gone now
with the smell of the shavin's. An' the ghosts of

79

their women rose in the smoke: all but my mother—
an' she only delayed long enough to give me the
back of her hand. By my soul, there in the middle
of the new mornin' she gave me the cold creeps
for burnin' the house.'

Charlie merely smiled.

'What'll we do about the rustic demand-notes?'
Mick challenged.

'Sell the house,' said Charlie without a pause.

'Oh, then, begod, the mother will be back,'
Mick said.

'Maybe she left the thought here before goin','
Charlie told him.

'Who'd buy it?' asked Mick.

'Them with shops in the street below.'

'For what use?'

'You should know that,' said Charlie.

'I never bothered my neck with home matters,'
Mick defended himself.

'Stripped of their insides, houses like this are
handy for stores,' Charlie explained.

'An' we can perch like a thrush on a hawthorn
bush, I suppose?'

'We'll sell it on condition that it shelters us while
we need shelter.'

'Will they buy it that way?'

'Half the houses in the lane are bought that way,'
said Charlie.

6

'Come away!' said Mick, making for the door.

They got twenty pounds for the house. Five

pounds satisfied the owners of the burned articles. Drink took the rest inside ten days. On the morning of the tenth day Charlie raised himself out of stupor, stood, swayed and fell face forward onto Mick's bed. Mick straightened him where he lay, listened at the sad mouth for breathing, felt for heart-beats in the big-boned vault of the chest. Satisfied that he was alive, Mick began to call in his ear and shake him at the shoulders, till Charlie stirred of his own accord. His eyes opened and humour gathered in them, taking time.

'I heard you over the way,' he told Mick.

'It must be wan hell of a distance,' Mick mumbled. 'How are you now?'

'Like I came back to know what time it was.'

'Time for a doctor.'

'Not till after nightfall,' said Charlie.

Mick stayed with him through the day, now and again brewing cups of tea for him in the battered tin on the recovered oil stove: not talking much and hardly being spoken to at all. He waited until night seeped in at the small window and settled in the crannies before he lit the candle. Then he went for the doctor.

The doctor, a young man in a hurry, had no reason to delay with his opinion. He took Mick aside and told him it was a matter of where he wished that his brother should die.

'How long will it be?' Mick asked.

'Longer than you can look after him here,' the doctor told him. 'Weeks, a month maybe.'

The doctor also knew his people.

'Look here,' he added, 'I can get him a bed. I

can't get him into hospital on the ticket. His being an incurable will mean . . .'

'I know, I know,' Mick cut in. He added: 'Do you mind goin' as far as the door, doctor, till I have a word with himself.'

The doctor went to the door as Mick returned inside the sacking. Mick walked up and down a few times, raking the boards with the look of offence in his small peevish eyes, as if the floor had swallowed his last threepenny bit. He sat on his bed and poked for the pipe inside the lining of his jacket. He frowned at the pipe as if he blamed it for hiding. He bit viciously on the chewed stem and lit a match. The match paused on the way to the pipe head. The match burned out in his fingers. He lit another match and lighted the tobacco with it in the leisurely way of the lead-up to a drink: the hurt had left his eyes.

'I suppose I'll have to poke out a supply of smokes for you first thing in the mornin',' he said. 'You'll want them in . . . that place.'

'Oh . . . that place,' echoed Charlie, with Mick's emphasis on the two words.

Mick spoke at length then, from a quick opening gradually taking time and sparing breath.

'We went there with my mother wan time, you remember. We were young lads, and she was young in her Sunday clothes. 'Twas a great thing to feel Sunday clothes in the middle of the week, or any ordinary day. She took us there that day: we were young and she was young herself in a Sunday bonnet and coat. She had a basket of things, with oranges on top. We wanted to do for so many of the oranges that she asked us was it we were sick or the neighbour in . . . that place.'

'That place . . .' said Charlie.

''Tis quare how you remember a thing,' said Mick. 'I remember she saying that day: it was a fine sunny day the way it is in my mind now— I remember she sayin' an' the sun shinin' on the world that it didn't matter; that it didn't matter at all that the old stock neighbour would go the rest of the way in that place. 'Tisn't where, but how, that matters, she told us. Then she put a smilin' eye on me an' said: 'The thing is, not to finish in jail, of course.' Thinkin' she saw me stealin' that other orange, I put it back. And she laughed out. And we laughed. We all laughed together. Then she gave us an orange each and said that was the last now, and no more: not to spoil the clane white collars now, and no more. 'Tis quare how you remember a thing.'

'The doctor is waitin' at the door,' Charlie reminded.

'Oh, be damned, yes,' said Mick.

He got to his feet, but he did not move away. After a pause he walked as far as the sacking.

'I suppose I'll tell him,' he said.

'I suppose,' said Charlie. 'Tell him that as a doctor he's a sound judge.'

Mick joined the doctor at the door.

'That'll be all right, doctor,' he said.

'I'll phone the ambulance and have him removed straight away,' the doctor decided. 'I can fill in the red tape in the morning.'

'Fill it in tonight, doctor,' Mick told him. 'An'

while you're at it fill out a form for me. You know the names. He's Charlie, I'm Mick. I'll call for mine tonight.'

'For—' the doctor began.

'That place,' said Mick.

With the last threepenny bit snuggled in the right peak of his waistcoat he followed the doctor down the lane and bought Charlie a packet of smokes for the road.

7

When the ambulance came Mick held the door of the house open for the driver and his helper to pass out with the prostrate Charlie on the stretcher. When Charlie was laid in the ambulance he went and hovered about the door. He could not make up his mind whether it was better that Charlie had either no breath or no mind to whistle. He called into the gloom of the cab, below the glow of gaslight through the high, square cab windows.

'Charleen.'

'Well?'

'Are you there?'

'I think so.'

'I'll see you tomorra.'

'If I'm not there I'll be elsewhere.'

'I'll bring a drop,' said Mick.

'You can launch me with it,' said Charlie.

The driver brought the engine to life. The helper entered the cab and closed the doors. The ambulance felt its way down the narrow place, bumping gently on the cobbles. Before it was out of sight Mick went back into the house. The dead smell of the place repelled any memories the walls might have huddled between them. He went beyond the sacking into the candle light. Apart from the candle flame the only bright thing in the small space was the statue: the too-bright blue of cloak and white of gown was toned by the dust, and in the soft light the gilt-gold of the rosary had the patina of the antique. The corkscrew put Mick in mind of a thirst he had no way of relieving. He snuffed the candle out, crushing the frail blossom of light with his fingers. Then he left the house to call on the doctor for his workhouse ticket.

Sky Is Plentiful

I never rightly understood the old man when he was there in the lane living, working, fighting an odd time with a man bigger than himself, or playing his tin whistle on a chair tilted over the back legs and braced by his shoulders against the hearth wall.

When I say the old man lived I don't mean that he had not yet died. There are people who have died long before they sigh themselves away on a last breath: the old man—my father—lived all the time. With his last breath he gave the word 'Right' up to my mother's hovering face. 'Right' was his word for acceptance or for challenge. 'Right' he said to the big man who wanted to stop words honed on the edge of his tongue on what the big lad called a daft idea and the old man called a principle. The other man was always bigger; men of the old man's small size were more cautious for being nearer to shoulders that would all but calm the drop in a spirit level at dead centre. The old man was a stone worker and big men are softer at the core than green stone or granite, but when stone had brought age to know his forties the big lads had their day.

I was said by my mother's view—I had not the wit then to see that she exaggerated to speed the moral—that his fighting arguments were sins against sense and dignity. Several times a week he was meeting Protestant Captain Martin in Carty's snug.

The Captain's skin and clipped beard, with their look of hoar frost and berries, gave him the cut of a superior Santa Claus in baggy tweeds. His eyes looked as if they never got over seeing sails vanish in steamer smoke like gulls in cloud, but because the sea at least was the same sea he remained a sailor, until the Navy decided that he was no longer seaworthy. He came home then to three dependent spinster daughters and had his own back, for their robbing him of even grandsons for the sea, by referring at all times to their Protestant household as 'The Nunnery'. But to eke out his pension for their genteel needs he forsook hot toddies for mulled porter, cigars for a big bay pipe on a galloping hoof, hotel lounges for pubs and parrots for pigeons.

In Carty's he and the old man would war with words until the very number of their disagreements stirred a common thought that sent hands in search of drinks and put minds to rest at a depth beyond depths sounded by too many too often. Then the Captain would stuff the big pipe-head with shag and ask for a tune on the whistle. The old man would take the whistle out of the coloured handkerchief in his inside pocket and play opera pieces, sea shanties, folk tunes with a hollow wind-sob of feeling, or the 'Blackbird', with the beat of the bramble under the sleek bird and the whirl of the song in the amber gorge.

After that they would have one for the road and part the best of friends, the old man to come home to the lane and the Captain to go to his orchard to scatter maize seed for his pigeons and pour water in the stone trough that he had had the old man chisel for them.

'In the sky they remind me of sails on the sea, Mac,' he told the old man one time. 'Gulls are better for that,' said the old man. 'Gulls won't be tamed and pigeons will be too tamed and overbred,' the Captain grumbled. 'My spoilt pigeons won't rise higher than my eave shoots. My toy sails are always in port and never at sea, like myself, always in port and never bloody anywhere. Don't you like pigeons, Mac?'

The old man did. The Captain told him that the brood pair mated for life. He liked that. Off his own bat he maintained that the pigeon was the one bird that lost nothing in grace or looks for being perched on a dung heap: and it was my own first pigeon that helped me on the way to my day-after-the-fair understanding of him.

*   *   *

I got that pigeon in the shell of an old granary, inside the lane archway, where pigeons came and went through the gold-dust of old grain by a hole in the slates. Street pigeons all, the low spread cloaks of flight they made were grey: sea grey, slate grey, old head grey in dim light, or blue smoke or mist or washwater blue, until Captain Martin's thoroughbreds after his death (to his last day he had liquor on his breath, a lash-lick to his tongue, rope welts in his palms and brine in his beard) missing his care in the shelter of the orchard, went for pot luck and royster in the granary.

Then the greys and blues of the flights began to have streaks of copper, bronze, amber, honey and white. In time the bright streaks narrowed in the flights, but began to show as a sheen or a graining, or both, in the colour of one in three of the separate birds. The one I got, with the aid of a ladder, out of a joist hole in the granary had the bare promise of copper among the grey first feathers.

It was a mid-June Saturday afternoon, the old man's pay day and half-day combined. Heat shimmered out of the round sun like sound from a bronze gong. It beaded the trout-speck freckles on my face so that I wore them like a mesh. Bread could have been browned on the cobble stones under my feet. I was lost in admiration of the pigeon and did not see the old man coming towards me at first, but I heard him.

For a small man he took a long step and hit the ground hard with it. Even as he was then, with the nailed boots off and the light Sunday boots on you would hear his step before another man's. He had

89

the good soft hat back-tilted so you could see his hair black giving ground to grey, curled hard in a close crop that would have been easy to work in stone. Clean shaven, except for his full moustache, his face had the furrows and colour of worn brown shoe leather and his eyes were as black as heel-ball.

His only offer to show was his great-grandfather's silver watch-chain, securing his grandfather's key-winder watch to his waistcoat. He looked what he was: a craftsman on his day off with new coin in his pocket. Over his shoulder I could see my mother in our second-storey window looking on the old man and at me with my pigeon. But not for anything would I have let her know I had seen her and not for all the world would the old man have let her discover that he knew she was there. And he did know, because one time it was he with the bare feet and his father with the watch and watch-chain, and his own mother in the window on pay day between two minds whether to rest easy with the good moment or worry right away about time to come.

'See my pigeon, Dad?' I asked. At rest he was a shy man. Even I made him shy out-of-doors and had always to speak first. 'So you robbed a nest?' he gave back. 'I left one and took one,' I said. 'The lad I left is all grey. This lad has copper in his feathers.' 'A pennyworth,' he said. 'Oh, more,' I argued. 'A penny-ha'penny so,' he said, 'but show him here to me.'

His hands, file rough in the palms, with a vein and sinew webbing on the backs that might have been plaited out of winter ivy by a creel maker,

90

were always crouched at the stone man's bred half-way between grip and caress: controlled power worth stating in stone that moulded it. The hands closed over my young pigeon in a way that would not have spoilt the wing-dust of a moth.

'He's a good one, Dan,' he said. 'He's game.' He let the wings fall out to full point. 'Them toy sails will go to sea, Dan. He's not afraid of anything.'

'You'd know it in his eye,' I said. 'You'd know it from his heart, Dan,' he corrected, 'beating sure and steady in the hollow of my palm as if it rested yet in the mother's breast mould you took it out of. He'll fly, Dan, surely.'

'Where, Dad?' I asked. 'High, Dan, because the sky is always plentiful, and always home, Dan, because even birds must come to earth. Here, show him to your mother now.'

I gathered my pigeon back on to the hot wool of my gansey and said 'So long.' He did not answer, nor did he move and I knew what was coming. It came too. 'Dan,' he called.

When I turned his back was to me. His right hand was hooked by his thumb to his trouser pocket. 'Well, Dad?' 'Here,' he said. Still looking away, he turned the hand palm up under his best coat tail. In the hollow was a shilling.

'Buy maize seed for that bird,' he said. 'It will strengthen the pinions and smoothen the feathers for clean flight. So long.' And that was the last coherent word I ever heard from him. I was too taken up with the young pigeon and the shilling to watch him go. But my mother in the window watched him out of sight. I went on into the two-

91

storey, white-washed house through the stone-flagged hall and up the nine steps of shaky stairs to the landing of the two rooms we had on rent from the Irishean who lived on the ground floor by herself.

* * *

Fifteen years previous, the Irishean had come inland from Dingle when she had lost her two sons to the sea and her daughter in marriage to a fisherman. She knew as many words of English as helped her to buy her food and snuff and to ask for her pension at the post office on Fridays. But to herself, in the house, she spoke Irish that matched every mood of the sea she crooned over or cursed, moaned to or bemoaned, but could never forget. It was as if there was a hollow in her where words broke and healed like sea sounds in a cave.

From the landing I went past the parent's bedroom into the living room that had a nook for my own narrow bed. My mother tried hard to make a fuss over my pigeon. 'But the mother bird will be looking for it in the nest, Dan, 'tis a shame for you,' she complained.

'When he's big he'll meet her in the sky,' I defended. ''Tis not the same,' she said, 'but 'tis a good thing too.'

She took the thrush cage down off the glass case for me and I spent the hours till bed time foraging among the tipped-up carts in the market place, stealing hay and straw from under the dreaming heads of donkeys tethered to the cart wheels, and buying tuppence-worth of maize seed at each of the town's six seed shops.

Day went out like a bank of new pennies, the light going as if door after door of the vaults were closed. But my mother was more interested in the closing of the pub doors at half-past ten, because the old man had not come home. By eleven he had not come home, so she made me take off my clothes and go to bed. Having looked at the pigeon and eased my mind about his comfort on the clean straw I went between the blankets. I pretended sleep because my mother liked that she alone would have the strain of waiting.

The small window framed the bit of June night that I could see about her head. The blue-black sky had stars in it like candles being breathed on. The air was still enough to let the musk smell of geranium leaves into me from the outer sill. On her knees, elbows on the inner sill, motionless, the mother might have been kneeling at a shrine. On or about every hour she rose and put a sod on the hearth and the fire turned over on its doze, shrugged and dozed away again. Each time she came and stood over me. I felt her hands raising the bed clothes off my shoulders and putting them back again the same as they were before. I could feel her look on my face as if her eyes had breathed it down. Then she went back and put her greying head into the icon of stars.

Below the rickety flooring the Irishean's flow of Gaelic breathed like a litany. Beyond the window the barking of a dog echoed more as the night emptied. I was in the shallows of sleep when I heard his step. My mother was leaning further out at the window to see him better as he passed under the gas lamps. Then I heard a moan from her that she tried to clench with her fists at her open mouth. But her movements were quick and sure when she struck and lighted the wick of the hanging oil lamp on the hob and shaped the light with a round-bellied globe. She took the lamp off the nail and went with it over the landing, down the stairs and along the hall to within a pace of the closed hall door. With my pants held by a fist on my middle I followed with my bare feet on her shadow. The old man came nearer with step and stumble. The Irishean's litany of Gaelic sounded like she was answering herself, as if she had to hear herself above wave upon wave.

Statue-still my mother stood inside the door and in her shadow I hardly dared to breathe while the step and stumble on the stones drew nearer through the flow and ebb of strong-throated Gaelic. Then the steps stopped outside the door. The lamp in the mother's hand was motionless through a pause that seemed a deal longer than it was because I held breath and heard heart-beats against taut ear-drums. I cried out as the door crashed open to show the old man. His good hat was gone and a gash on his crown showed in his thick hair like a crevice. There was blood on either side of his face and on the shoulders of his jacket. He must have lain unconscious where it happened for a time because the blood had crusted to the purple-black of sloes. The watch hung loose on the silver chain and where he swayed in the light it swung like a pendulum of time vacant in eternity.

He was not conscious yet or he would not be there in the lamplight with his face misshapen from kick or blows or both, because never before had he come home without getting skilled help to hide the worst. From his eyes I would have known that he was not fully there anyhow. They were empty. Then he moved forward under the raised lamp. My mother followed close. I was on her heels.

At the foot of the stairs he stopped, looked up and almost crumpled. My mother's hand went out but his right hand reached out to push it away, as if it was a thought he had thought himself before. Then he seemed to suddenly find his feet because his body grew up from them to straightness. His head took on the game cock of his best days.

'Right,' he said. Then he went on up the stairs and into the bedroom, to fall face first into full unconsciousness on the bed.

During twelve hours there was the doctor's head-shake, my mother's waiting for the old man to pass behind the glazed opes of his eyes, his pause as he passed to look at her and say 'Right', the stone man having a sea dirge ullagoaning in the voice of the Irishean, and the pigeon gone as cold in my mind as a sculped dove on a tomb.

During twelve weeks there were the dove cote wrought for my pigeon by a craftsman in wood, the stone trough brought from Captain Martin's three daughters by their gardener, and the arrival of the daughters themselves to give my mother her first jobs at the dressmaking she took up to keep home and rear me.

I know now why I had that grudge against the pigeon but on the way to knowing there were a few confusions. Kids are quick enough to hop-step into stride with life away from the full stop of a grave. Any grave. But I brought with me hate for the man or men who had killed the old man.

The mother sensed a change in me since the old man went. She would complain that it was she and the Irishean who had to feed and water the pigeon. Part of a plan, no doubt, to stop the youth in one from curdling. I think if she could have played a tune on the dusty whistle on the hob she would. Whatever else had colour in our drab place was hers and of woman—the geranium blossoms, the small red lamp under the big picture of the Sacred Heart, even the wild flowers in the vases that flanked the light, because I brought them home under my gansey when I was told.

There again I would say that the daily call for fresh flowers was to send me away to places she knew I liked because I had talked so often about them: places of river and hill, lake and mountain, heron or lark in sun or in rain. They were out and about that town in renowned riches and they cost nothing to see and only thought to feel. But when I came back she was troubled again that when I spoke of what I saw it was to answer her questions and what I felt I never told her at all. The pigeon she took to be her main hope for cure of what ailed me and she used him for all he was worth.

One day she heeled up on the treadle of the sewing machine and told me to go and have a look at the bird. 'There is nothing the matter with him,' I said.

I had had the bit to eat after school and was waiting for Eddie McConnell to whistle me away to a game of handball in the alley of the airing court of the Mental Hospital. The school alleys were forbidden to us after school hours. The Mental Hospital alley was forbidden to us too but it was good, and anywhere was better than school.

'The dump pits at the back are alive with cats, Dan, and your bird is one to fly low,' the mother argued. 'That's what's wrong with him,' I said. 'What do you mean?' she asked. 'Only that's what's wrong with him,' I said.

She thought that out. She was nearer to a core now and she knew it. She was nearer still with the next thing she said and nearer the centre than I. 'The bird is young, son,' she said, 'and our world is so low. There is nothing higher than a two-storey house and no wall higher than a dump pit dyke.'

Her fourteen years in America before she married solved for her the Irish riddle between ditch and dyke. She called a tap a faucet and a Z a Zee.

'Our world is not far from the ground, Dan,' she added. 'Sky is plentiful,' I said, half to myself. That brought a pause. 'Dad used to say that,' she reminded. 'I know,' I said.

There was a pause longer that time. She ran a bobbin to fullness before she spoke again. 'I was only thirteen years when I went to Boston with the emigrants,' she said, 'working in the woollen mill and living near it in a kind of cellar of the city and not nice. I felt like an ant under a stone and lonely. Then, one Sunday I went with a lot of others for a trolley ride out of the city. It was a big adventure, Dan.'

I used to revel in stories of this kind and she knew that too. She paused to see how I was taking this one. I felt mean because I couldn't warm to her telling the way I used to. 'The last trolley stop put us where the city ended and the land began. There were orchards, I remember. Every tree drooped with weight of ripe red apples and yellow apples. But what I saw was the sky. I looked up at it, and into it, and cooled in it as if the blue was sea and the clouds were foam and the birds were flying upside down. It was nice, Dan.'

I felt that whatever she was hunting in me was hiding in me and I couldn't find it even for myself. I looked at my bare toes, felt the pause curl about them and look up at me with her eyes, and I tried to rise out of the chair. 'Listen a little more, Dan,' she said. 'It won't be long. When I came back to the mill and the boarding house and the cellar again I remembered every day to look up at the sky and it was the same sky. Sky is plentiful but we must see it. So, maybe, if you took the pigeon with you into the country he'd see the sky and remember ever after that the same sky was here too.'

'Cod,' I said. That really hurt her. It was a short word and easily out, but it was out and there it was. I didn't feel her eyes through the pause that time.

'Your Dad said "cod" about many things,' she said, 'but never about that. When I told him what

I told you now was the first time I heard him say
"sky is plentiful".'

She waited for a word of answer or comment
but I had none to make. Then the machine whirred
like angry crickets and I left the room. I went over
the landing and down the stairs into the hallway. I
opened the yard door by chinks to take the pigeon
unawares.

He wasn't a bad bird to look at. He had the cheek
that would age into pride with a burgeoned breast,
spread tail and the full bass of the croon that would
deepen down from mouse-squeak immaturity. The
copper was still a penn'orth in the feathers but the
grey was deepening to blue, the throat sheen rippled
in the light, the legs were clawed crimson and the
eye amber and fit for setting by a goldsmith. The
cote was hanging on the back wall of the house
from a brad that had held one end of a clothes line.
I stepped into the yard.

On the ledge of the cote he squatted, preening
the wing pinions. Feathers floated in the trough
water where he had washed a time ago. When he
saw me he rose up to full reach and cheeked me
with one eye and the other. Then he lay on the
air under spread wings and cut the loops of an
eight of flight out over the dump pits and back to
the ledge. But never for an instant was he higher
than an eave.

I had tried to make him rise. I had gone the
length of hurtling stones under his flights to drive
him high but he mocked me with capering scoops
of flight and fall, out of line but never out of range.
And there he was back on the ledge again, shaping,

trying to sell his ha'porth of coppers to the sun as pure gold, trying to win my interest with slitting of a silence full of sunlight (that smelled faintly of dump pits) with the slender zither pinging of his wings.

Eddie McConnell whistled in the hallway just then and I brought the pigeon with me. 'What are you doing with that?' he asked. 'Taking him with me,' I said. 'Is it a homer?' he asked. 'That's what I want to know,' I said and we left it at that.

The Mental Hospital is on a hill beyond the town and big enough to fool people into thinking it the town itself. The stone of it looked as if it needed a deluge to wash it down. The windows of it had very many small panes of glass and there was never a time when a window had all the panes or a minute without a patient's face mope-eyed in the light or a hand throwing pellets of paper through the space where a pane should have been. The ball alley was in the men's airing court west of the hospital. There was nothing between the patients and escape during airing time except a six-foot iron railing and attendants pacing each his own short stretch of railing like policemen on the beat.

The court was a field but what grass had the courage to grow near that ugly mass of masonry was scabbed with patches walked bare by patients' nailed boots and pocked with small and big-enough holes where patients had scooped or kicked little graves for dead memories or for the want of anything at all to do. The big, plain alley, midway and inside the railing on the western end of the court, had no back wall, so that patients could watch attendants play during airing time. It looked like a bomb-damaged stone house that someone had healed up with old plaster. The whole court looked like a bombed area.

We got there about four on the late August afternoon. We climbed the railings by gripping the loop head to every first and third bar (the loop arched over the spike on each centre bar, on the principle that an escaped patient caused less up-roar in a Board Room than a dead one) and walked with our bare feet up the centre bar.

I put the pigeon on the railings and he perched there as unconcerned as a hen on a roost feeling night wean light away out of the coop. I snatched him off the perch and walked with him to the centre of the court.

'What are you up to?' Eddie asked me. He was long and thin, with limp hair, and all his thoughts ended in a question and stayed there. 'I want him to see the sky,' I said. 'Is he blind?' asked Eddie. 'We'll see,' I said. 'Is this a good place for notions like that?' Eddie asked. 'Go to hell,' I said. 'I'll go out into the alley and loosen up,' he said. Not until he was away and I was alone with the pigeon did I feel that the old man was with me. When I looked at the sky I thought of the mother. It was high and clear of cloud in the dome, a deep blue womb, warm with light lambent on gull wings. Lark specks quivered high over the farm fields like soot motes blown up out of the fire of the westering sun. I showed the pigeon the sky. I willed him hard to see it and feel its vastness wooing for his wings.

Then I flung him skywards. His wings beat wildly at house-eave's reach, fluttered for balance and skimmed down the air to the scabbed turf. Eddie's laughter echoed hollow in the valley. I turned my back on the bird and walked head down towards the laughter.

I worked off part of my venom against the pigeon in knocking the ball hard and fast, low and high against the drab concrete. Eddie had height and reach and a kind of dogged endurance that made a game with him close but always a winning one. That evening I played with an intensity that made for a nervy pallor instead of heat and sweat and Eddie broke the silence several times with—'Anything the matter with you?' and I shook my head and buried another ace on the bottom stone or knocked it well over his head. 'Where's that pigeon?' he asked me once. 'I don't care a damn,' I told him.

I remember it began when he tossed a long ball down the centre. I hit it hard and low to a butt that left him no chance even to get his toe to it because there was no hop. I was moving in to deal and he was coming out to play at the end of the alley when I saw his face stretch in terror that lit his eyes. 'Holy God!' he cried.

When I turned about there was a knock in my chest like a hammer-top. Half the court was full of patients, walking towards us with myopic eyes, their hands hanging below short coat cuffs and feet striding in nailed boots. One or two in strait-jackets looked like part clad divers without a helmet and all strode towards us like men stalking a life on lynch law. That was how it seemed to me. One man with the peak of his cap over his left ear and eyes grey-cold ran at us. 'Run,' I shouted to Eddie. 'Jesus,' he cried and ran out of the alley and back to the railings.

His being ahead of me heightened my terror of the pounding boots behind me. Eddie was up and over the railing before I started to climb. 'He's coming, hurry!' he cried.

I missed my foothold a few times but in the end I fell face forward onto the avenue as the railings rattled from the force of the patient's run against it. I heard the too-loud lunatic laughter of the patients before I could pick myself up. I heard the more measured laughter join it and when I turned around I saw the patient and the attendant in his white coat, both as breathless as I was.

'That will teach ye lads to leave us our alley to ourselves,' the attendant said. 'Little snipes, they were,' the patient said, 'little frightened snipes skittering out of cover above a gun. Little ladeens, t'was a shame.'

'Well, blast you anyway,' Eddie said on his first even breath. The patient laughed again and the attendant put a calming hand on his shoulder. 'You did your work, Pats. That's enough, boy. Enough,' he said.

But just then the whole court full of patients started a gale of crazy laughter on their own. The cause was my pigeon. The patients were chasing it from perch to perch along the north railing, their arms looking extra long in the shank from the shortness of the sleeves of their thick suits. The nearest hand to each new perch grabbed at the blue bird

103

that rose on the full spread of white lined wings out of reach to sway away to another perch further down the railing. In the brown shapeless suits that somehow smelt collectively of smoke-damp they hunted the bird, grabbing at it with great hands on long red shanks of wrist.

The white coats rushed here and there among the brown, pushing, holding, knocking as the laughter rose and the great hands reached out of the mass and grabbed at the bird that rose in white lined flights always out of reach away to perch again, to rise and sway again along the railings.

Somehow the old man was in that laughter-mad pursuit and I was watching, waiting for the kill.

'That's my pigeon,' I said to the white coat near me. 'He'll be all right,' he said. 'I'm going for him,' I said.

I made to climb back over the railings but he put a hand on my shoulder that weighed heavier than lead. I fell away under it and ran down the railing to climb again. The white coat followed along, place after place I tried. I began to cry with rage and frustration. The white coat got into a kind of a frenzy. On my sixth or seventh attempt to get over he hit me with the knuckles of a big fist over the ear. I fell stunned to the ground and Eddie asked was I all right.

I had to fight through tears and daze to get the place in focus. Through the swirl several times I found even keel and each time I began to notice something. It was this. Each time the pigeon rode a reaching hand he rose higher above the railings. Sitting on the ground I watched the brown mass of

104

humanity laugh and grab and saw the pigeon rise higher than the eaves he knew. Then suddenly when he was beyond tree height he began to soar. I watched him rise, and watching, the fears fell away and the white coat was forgotten as I saw him soar into the womb of sky.

The flight fountained up and up through crow-flap and gull scroll until the white of the wing linings turned silver in the light. Higher and higher he rowed the air with the silver wings till there was nothing above him but larks. You could imagine the wings feeling the fall of lark-song to hush on fields to dew on grass, to breast of mate and warmth of scalding. And high between the highest gull and lowest lark my pigeon was a silver flash that suddenly ceased to circle and sped arrow-straight towards the town.

* * *

As I picked myself up I felt the silence. The brown mass and the white coats stood with their faces raised silent to the sky. I looked back for the wings of my pigeon and they weren't there. I began to run. Eddie followed with his long legs, shouting: 'Where are you going? What are you doing?' But I didn't answer. He ran with me until he could run no longer. I shouldn't have been running that long without stopping but I was. My body seemed to have made a rhythmic habit of running, my lungs a rhythmic pain of breathing.

Running into the town from the Asylum was down-hill work. When the heat and sweat swelled

105

the blood in my head I felt the bump big and painful over my right ear where the attendant had hit me. I ran on down Rock Road, down Meara's Hill, down High Street, through Main Street, up Henn Street, across the Square and down New Lane where I lived. The mother was watering the geraniums on the window sill. When she saw me she showed fright in her face that for a moment was a shadow of the way she looked the night the old man dragged death all the way home in spite of itself.

She went in from the window and was standing inside the door when I turned in at the hall.

'The pigeon,' I said.

'What about him, son?'

'I took him up Asylum Hill. He flew right up into the sky. Then he flew right down towards town. I think he's home.'

'We'll see,' she said.

We ran down the hall, threw open the door into the yard. But there was no pigeon.

'He's not home yet,' she said.

'He should be,' I said.

''Tis a long flight, Dan,' she said.

'I ran as far,' I said.

'You knew the way,' she reminded me. 'We'll wait here in the doorway till he comes.'

Beyond the dumps—the width of a livery stable beyond—was a storehouse roof and over the roof was the crown of a beech tree. The sun bedded down red into the west beyond the tree and the crown of leaves was like a brazier. We stood motionless in the doorway silent for minute upon minute of waiting, looking ahead. Then of a sudden the pigeon sped out of the brazier tree of skyfire like a flame, to swoop low over the dump walls and glide up to claw to a perch on the ledge of the cote.

'Right,' said the mother and the word was in my mind to say.

I felt her smile before I looked up into it. When I smiled back I felt the bruise over my ear where I was hit but I kept on smiling anyway. She was still smiling when she turned her face from me. But for a long while after I only saw her back.

.

Like Father, Like Son

Danny Coyle was a cross that teacher and pupils had to carry in our class at the monastery school. Except for him we were a lot of honourable hardchaws. He was a slyboots. We rough and tumbled between us for survival; he stepped down from his nine years of age after school to bully innocents of eight and seven and so on down the line. And when lads of his age or older came between him and his victims with a boot on the rear or a punch on the kisser he wailed out—'I'll tell my Da!'

And most of the trouble about him was that same Da. Jack Coyle was easily the strongest man in our town or the country round it. He was so broad you hardly noticed how tall he was: six feet and an inch or two. His huge hands at the end of long arms were hung by his thumbs to his belt when he wasn't working. He earned a living at the sawmill where he tossed chunks of tree around like kindling. A showoff.

He'd as soon lift a barrel of porter onto a pub counter as drink it. But now, at forty-five or so, he opted for the ease of drinking and left the lifting to youngsters who tried to match feats of his they had heard about. The old grey suit he wore on Sundays he covered with an overall for work in the weekdays. His cap sloped to his right ear and his moustache bristled no matter what humour he was in. Give him his due, he was a quiet enough man till he was roused. And Danny was the rouser.

Outside of the classroom Danny meant 'I'll tell my Da' when he said it. He knew the way Jack doted on him as the son who came by special delivery from the Almighty after six daughters in a row. So he went to him with the names of the lads who stopped his bullying of others with a kick or a cuff in the right place. And Jack called on their fathers after work, flexing his muscles, opening and closing his fists at their doorsteps, warning them to control their sons if they didn't want their very own heads knocked off.

And believe me, no one's father wanted his son to be the cause of a visit from Jack Coyle. Even granted that it was holy and wholesome to save kids from being pushed about by a bully, they felt it would be wiser for their sons to win and wear haloes well clear of the Coyles. That meant that Danny went on strutting between whinges in Jack's shadow. So it would be true to say that the trouble with Danny was his father, the trouble with the father was his son. Like father like son in a way, with the father the better.

Inside the classroom when Danny talked of telling his Da, it was our teacher Tom Coffey who was at the receiving end of his barbs. Tom was a rawboned frame of a man with a mop of the kind of fair hair that brought freckles with it into his late twenties. It left him looking boyish when he was barely on the right side of thirty, especially when his lopsided smile made one of its rare appearances inside monastery walls. He was stroke oarsman for the Valley crew in regattas on the lakes that made our town world famous. He played good football and cycled eight miles every morning to the monastery from Beaufort, a scattered village with houses and shops hidden in trees on the banks of the Laune.

The long-drawn six feet of him had no chance to be anything but fit. His hands made pens and pencils and pieces of chalk look smaller than they were and when he was driven to use the cane you felt it all the way to the marrow in your palms. 'Do your homework. In class keep your eyes and ears open and your mouth shut,' was his code and the cane came your way when you stepped out of line. Fair enough.

In his favour too was the fact that he was the only layman on the school staff. All the rest were monks and anyone who was taught by monks will tell you it was always at the back of his mind that monks were neither priests nor people. Priests in personal sacrifice went up Calvary all the way. Monks stopped half way and could go home any time they felt like it. Laymen like Tom Coffey had to put up with the world like the rest of us. They

110

were some of our own and their faults, like our own, were as public as washing.

All told, Coffey was a fair man who gave you a square deal and got an honest hand back from everyone.

Except Danny. And it was the third part of Coffey's code that brought matters to a head between the pair of them. The third rule told you that if you were late for school you had to bring a note from your mother or father to explain why you weren't in the yard when the bell rang.

Danny was a half-hour late when he brazened into the room on a Monday morning that sent sunlight pouring through the tall peaked monastery windows. The sun gave the only brightness that morning. Coffey had the hang-dog look of a man who did too much celebration of a win on the lake for the Valley the day before. He was licking his lips and not liking the taste. Any smiles he owned he left at home.

And it was then that Danny walked in, letting the heavy door shut with a clatter behind him. Coffey never took his eyes off him as he strutted to his seat, dropped the bag at his feet and looked at his well chewed fingernails. Bravado.

Coffey was still holding chalk at the blackboard when he said quietly: 'Where were you till this hour of the day, Coyle?'

'I was drawing water to shave my father,' said Danny, cool as always before the pay-off.

'You make it sound as if you should make a contract job of it. He must have a lot of face,' said Coffey.

'The pump is a long way up the lane from our house,' Danny explained.

'And that makes it a long way back of course. Did you wait to see him shave all that face?' Coffey asked, dead-pan as you please.

'Only the half of it,' said Danny. 'When he cut himself with the oul' open razor he told me to get the hell out of there.'

'And only half the show kept you a half hour late for school?' said Coffey, still nice and quietly.

'That and the walk here after,' Danny told him.

'With the note?' said Coffey.

'What note?' said Danny.

'The note you asked him to write for you to account for your being late.'

'Oh, that!' said Danny. 'He said he'd send that along later by carrier pigeon.'

'And get the pigeon to write it for him as well, I'm sure, but he wouldn't like us to know that, would he?' said Coffey.

'He wouldn't give a damn,' Danny rapped back. 'My Da don't give a damn about anything.' Then he added: 'Or anybody' looking Coffey straight in the eye.

'Unfortunately I have to give a damn about you,' said Coffey. He reached for the cane at the back of the blackboard. 'Come up here,' he added.

Danny lost some of his cockiness with every step. By the time he was within cane's reach of the teacher he was beginning to cringe. Then he slipped into his familiar routine of putting on the boy martyr's face to look up at the torture stick. Then he whinged. 'Hold out your right hand,' said

112

Coffey.

Danny's way of doing that was to put out his palm under cover of his elbow, where he kept darting it in and out like a stoat in a burrow while Coffey tried to get a shot at it. He struck air three times before he scored a direct hit on the wrong part of the hand: Danny's wrist.

Danny's howl hit the black oak rafters. He danced on one leg with the wrist wrapped in his armpit. 'I'll tell my Da,' he screamed. He had turned his back on Coffey and was facing us when he stole a look at the wrist. When he saw the red weal across the white skin the war cry about his Da had the true ring of outrage. 'I'll tell my Da,' he screamed up into the long man's face and Coffey, who hadn't seen the livid cane mark, said in his country drawl: 'You're always promising to do that, Danny.'

'But this time I'll bloody-well do it!' Danny shouted over his shoulder as he scampered for the door, tugged it open and slammed it after him in a way that echoed in the monastery.

There was a silence before Coffey asked us: 'What was the new dimension in aid of?' and top of the class Con Nolan told him: 'You drew red on his wrist, sir.'

Coffey paused before he said, 'I wouldn't have hit his wrist if he hadn't played hide-and-seek with his palm.'

For the next two hours he took us through Mathematics and English with a few new twists off the boring routine. He was that kind of teacher: good. Then the bell rang at noon for the lunchtime break and we filed out through a porch as stone cool and empty as a mortuary.

The wide expanse of concrete yard was white with sun and hot as an oven. It had a shed, a handball alley and a lavatory that reeked with the piss of generations. Crows and gulls perched on eaves gawking at the crusts and crumbs the lads shed around them as they wolfed through milk and sandwiches. Finches and sparrows were spry enough to pick about the boys' feet where they stood around or sat on the warm concrete with their backs against walls.

It was a noon for siesta, but four of the senior lads were playing handball. Their shouts were finding echo in the hollow of the alley. Two monks were on the lunchtime watch. Tiny old Brother Eolan with snuff powder brown on the breast of his black habit was reading near the gate; a white handkerchief on his head to keep his bald skull from scorching. Brother Mark, the choirmaster, barrel-shaped as befitted a singer whose voice could make windows rattle, was in the peaked porch doorway; yawning. Tom Coffey had his bicycle upside down under our classroom window fixing a puncture.

The scene was so peaceful that the roar of 'Where's Coffey!' from the gate was a shock to us all. Sound and movement seemed to stop on the instant, except for the rubber ball bouncing loose from the alley and Coffey poking with a spanner at the bicycle. By that time Jack Coyle was walking on his own shadow towards Coffey: thumbs stuck in his belt, steely heels all but knocking sparks off the yard, Danny dancing in attendance like a pup on a lead.

'Are you Coffey?' he said to the back of the man bending over the bicycle.

'Mister Coffey inside the school walls,' Tom said without turning.

'I mister no man,' said Jack. 'Turn around till I talk to you.'

'So far I haven't seen you,' Tom told him in his country drawl. 'I'd like if it stayed that way.'

'I want to talk to you about my son,' said Jack.

'That's different,' said Tom, turning slowly.

When they stood face to face Jack snarled: 'Who the hell gave you the right to cut my son to pieces with a cane?'

'The pieces came together soon enough I see,' said Tom, glancing at Danny, who was hugging himself with satisfaction.

'I could take you to law,' said Jack. 'But I'll deal out my own justice by knocking your bloody head off.'

'I'm afraid I can't let you do that,' said Tom. 'Teachers are useless without heads in the way that you'd be useless without hands.' And the lopsided smile was there for the first time that morning.

He was raising his right hand to lift a lick of hair out of his eye when Jack hit him on the temple. It was a vicious blow that all but knocked him back over the bicycle.

'You shouldn't have done that,' he said, righting himself.

'You shouldn't have done the other,' said Jack, hitting out again.

But this time Coffey took the blow on his left forearm and let Jack have his right fist on his stained teeth. Jack looked as much surprised as offended. 'Now you did it,' he hissed as he drove forward with fists flailing. Youth and the fitness of an athlete were on Coffey's side. He took most of the blows on his arms, sidestepped others and swung his head side to side for safety in a way that would do credit to a trained scrapper. Needless to say, all of the two hundred pupils in the yard had formed a ring around the two men, a ring that moved with them as each man in turn drove the other back towards the alley.

Blow after blow the two exchanged, all of them heavy, some of them sickeningly so. A left jab from Jack raised a bump on Coffey's forehead. A right from Coffey split Jack's moustache dead centre of the bristles and the taste of his own blood made Jack wilder than ever. By now we knew that youth was locked with prime in an epic. Danny was dancing and shouting and the rest of us were giving tongue in the raw excitement. It went on and on, with sweat running into their eyes, down their noses, dripping off their chins onto their chests. Their shirts were stained with it, Coffey's flaming hair was wet with it. Jack's cap was stuck to his temples with it. You could smell it.

And it was when a blow of Jack's drew blood from Coffey's nose that Brother Mark barrelled his bulk between them shouting: 'This is gone far enough.' He gripped Coffey by the wrists and said: 'Have sense, Tom, you could lose your job on this.' Coffey said: 'Better lose my job than my manhood.'

116

Mark said 'Oh, heavens' in vexation and Coffey said 'Oh, hell' in frustration. Jack said: 'Let him loose in God's name before my fire goes out.'

'He's right, Mark, let go of my wrists,' said Coffey, and when Mark hung on he said: 'Look, do you want it on my slate that I hit a religious?' As Mark hesitated he added: 'Can't you see that if I back down no teacher will ever again be respected in this school, monk or layman.' That clinched the issue for Mark. He stepped back to let the two men tear into each other again with a venom made fresh by the break.

With blow after blow they belted each other into the alley where knuckle knocked louder on bone. Coffey's fists were beating on the drum of Jack's chest and getting sound out of it. Jack's round-the-house swings were finding Coffey's ears. In a kind of last stand slog, the fitness of the younger man was giving him the edge when little Brother Eolan swept the handkerchief off his head and darted between them like a little old cur between mastiffs. 'In God's name, stop!' he cried in his reedy voice.

'You'll get hurt, Eolan,' said Coffey kindly. 'You'll get killed,' said Jack with no kindness at all. 'Would you waste a blow on me?' said Eolan to Jack whose fists hung limp by his sides. '*You* could kill me with a finger,' he told Coffey. '*You* could kill me with a finger nail,' he told Jack. 'Go on, go ahead, I won't stop you.' And with Eolan looking up at him like a willing martyr, Jack said: 'I won't start, small man.'

Eolan jerked like a clockwork toy as he faced each man in turn with the handkerchief raised as if

117

it were a flag of surrender. 'I know you wanted to prove yourself to your son,' he told Jack. 'I know you wanted to make teaching safe in this place for another generation,' he told Coffey.

Then he stepped back to look at them both and said: 'Each of ye has proved his point to the hilt. Ye don't have to go to last breaths or death's doors or drive nails into coffins to make testimony. What do ye say to my calling it a draw, a draw with honour after a fair fight, what do ye say?'

Then the little tich made his master move. Without waiting for their answer he raised his palms to the yardful of silent faces and said: 'We'll call it a draw lads, won't we?' At the top of our voices we all answered 'Yes!'

The two battered men stood looking at each other without a word. We held breath. Then Jack broke the silence.

'No man ever stayed with me for so long,' he said.

'I had a notion I could overstay,' Coffey told him.

'I couldn't throw you out,' Jack said.

'I'll go now of my own accord,' Coffey said. 'I have a bike to fix.' His smile on a sore face was more lopsided than ever.

'Wait,' said Jack. He shuffled in his nailed boots, looked at his fist as if he never saw it before, closed a bruised eye and looked at Tom Coffey with the other. 'Any man who went so far to prove a point must be honest,' he said. 'Any time Danny won't do what you think is good for him, you tell me.'

'I'll do that,' said Coffey.

'Good luck to you now,' Jack told him.

'God speed,' said Coffey.

Jack walked away out of the yard with Danny in tow. Tom Coffey went back to his bicycle. Mark returned to the porch with all the yawns knocked out of him. Small Eolan put the handkerchief back on his head, opened his book and soon was reading as if nothing had happened.

It only remains to say that the next time Danny was called to the cane Coffey told him: 'And don't say you'll tell your Da, or I'll tell him for you. He told me so himself.' Then taking a leaf out of Eolan's book he turned to the class and said: 'Didn't he, lads?' And we answered 'He did!' in a chorus. But the lopsider was back on his face when he turned back to Danny. 'I owe you a let-off for that bruise on your wrist, Danny. Go back to your seat.'

Danny put on a brave show of no surrender as he walked back to the empty seat. He stood at the desk and looked defiance at all of us before he sat down at last. But he never said 'I'll tell my Da,' in that room ever after.

Pictures In A Pawnshop

Jack is with us still, thank God, but Joe Jack has taken the only knock that ever put him down to stay down, God rest him. Jack was a man when Joe Jack was a boy. Joe Jack caught up with him later. They were butties together in that part of the town known as Below. The Bridge without a bridge that was ever known there to be below, and a few of the boys below the bridge were playing on the town's football team for the county championship in Tralee that war-time Sunday. The pair wanted to be at that match, twenty-one miles away.

Labouring life and fight broke Joe Jack's face into pieces and time in a hurry took a rough and ready gamble in putting it together again. The gamble came off in a half and half of knuckle-buster and rogue kid. Far at the end of a great-muscled arm his clenched fist looked fit to crush stones before it opened to spill coin—when it had coin—on froth among tall glasses with workmates, and the same from them, and the same again, and one for the singer, and one for the song, and one for yourself, Mick, and one for the road, until the light went out in the mirrors and it was mind the step after that. His feet were tortured by a more than six-foot spread of eighteen stone.

Jack does not drink, but he would back a horse at a ploughing match; and because horses have no part in this story they must give way to the school kids who gathered at his shop door and called down the steps: 'Count us, Jack.' Light had been ebbing in Jack's eyes, and now dimness was at arm's length from him.

'How many are ye?' he would say, coming up to the blur of colours in the door frame (it was mostly girls who went to school through the street).

'We're three, Jack.'

'A one, and a two, and a two and a three, counts out a tune that you'd dance with glee,' Jack would say, sparking with his nailed boots on the flagstones.

'We're five now, Jack,' a voice might come, with fresh colours to the blur.

'A one, and a two, plus a three, makes five; if ye're late for school, ye'll be flayed alive,' Jack would make up, and the soap-shiny faces would light in mock alarm and scream away schoolwards.

When Joe Jack came to him, the Saturday evening before that match in Tralee, with a tale of woe and a scowl, Jack said: 'Get yourself a few school kids, Joe Jack, and I'll count you.'

''Tis nuthin' to laugh at,' Joe Jack growled.

'Sit down, man, and tell us,' said Jack.

So the pair sat on the shutterless greengrocer's window as an August dusk came up the street to them.

'There's a world war on, so there's no trains to Tralee,' said Joe Jack, in disgust. 'There's no cars to hire, because there's no petrol to buy, and there's a law to say a car journey must have a life to save. For love or money there's no seat idle in the few cars that are taking the chance, and my feet are red-raw from walking.'

'I must see that match,' said Jack.

'If I have to walk it,' said Joe Jack.

'I seen desperate men with wheels in search of bicycles and men with bicycles in search of wheels,' Joe Jack said. 'A wagonette that didn't get a day out since Parnell is going to get a day out tomorra. I seen hens cooshed out of ould sidecars and six men wanting right-go-wrong to hire a hearse.'

'A splendid idea,' said Jack.

'Only the owner roared back that he might have to go there himself in it.'

''Twas true for the man,' said Jack.

'I seen stray donkeys lifted off ditches,' said Joe Jack. 'Big dogs got in dread they might be saddled, so they dropped tails and ran all roads.'

'You tell it well,' said Jack.

'Men are prodding the dump pit with crowbars for car parts and Guards are doing duty by all petrol pumps,' said Joe Jack, in a kind of relished melancholy. 'Ould women, in terror, are shawling paraffin oil cans into holes in ould walls for safekeeping, and chemists have a shotgun on all barrels of olive oil and linseed oil.'

122

'Only natural,' Jack got in.

'The only thing safe is tap, well or lake water,' said Joe Jack, 'and that's only because no wan have a steam engine to make it worth his while going in search of a man with an ould pair of tracks. The town, in wan word, is mad this minute.'

A silence settled between the pair. The cider smell of apples from Jack's fruit counter brought Joe Jack's thirst to the boil in spittle.

Then: 'I must see that match,' said Jack.

'If I have to walk it,' said Joe Jack.

Then suddenly Jack said: 'That's a bargain.'

'What is?'

'That we'll walk it.'

'Done,' said Joe Jack, easing his weight to his feet.

When they had made arrangements for Mass and meeting, Joe Jack went a few doors down to Mother's snug and Jack got his shutters to toe the line by touch, his little ebbing of light full out now in the dark of the shop. And where there was light again there was Sunday.

During that Sunday there were times when the tar road to Tralee looked like a scrap-heap on the crawl to new quarters. A man with a three-speed gear on his bicycle could look down on the neighbours, and the odd man with a car felt he might be lynched by the rabble. One of the few wheeled rigs not used was the hearse, and only because an old footballer who should have known better, mistimed his last kick. But from early morning Jack and Joe Jack were going the mountain road by Firies.

Jack was fearful for Joe Jack's feet and Joe Jack

had fears for Jack's old heart. They fell into the habit of inviting each other to stand-easy on hilltops or sit on the brow of the road when Joe Jack had made sure there was no one looking. Jack called the first halt on Madam's Height and faced about towards the valley, with the town and the lakes in it.

'There's a view,' he said, waving his ash plant in the general direction.

'The view!' said Joe Jack, startled.

Jack tilted his head back until he was blinking skywards.

'No wind, blue air, white light,' he told himself. Then he blinked straight down into the valley. 'The Reeks, Tomies, Torc, Mangerton: they're puce under blue with the white of cloud in it, and the lakes are as smooth as well water.'

'Hey!' cried Joe Jack.

'So there's two of it all,' said Jack. 'Only wan is upside down, so you don't know if 'tis on your head or your legs you're standing.'

'I don't know,' said Joe Jack.

'There's a boat off Innisfallen like a fly on a mirror,' Jack said.

'There is,' cried Joe Jack.

'That'll be Son Leary, bound for the mouth of the Laune,' said Jack. 'That fellah would go fishing if all belonging to him was at a Kerry All-Ireland in Croke Park.'

'I'm off,' said Joe Jack.

'Where?'

'I wouldn't travel another peg of the road with a fraud. You can see as good as I can,' Joe Jack growled.

124

'When I could I couldn't see as clear,' said Jack. 'All my pictures now are framed, hanging in my head like in a pawn shop.'

'But look here,' said Joe Jack.

'I'm done with looking now for another year,' Jack told him, adding: 'How's the feet?'

'I'm no fraud,' growled Joe Jack. 'If I could hang 'em without hanging myself, they'd be hanging somewhere. I bet if there was a shilling on the road you'd see that, too.'

And arguing the toss about Jack's sight livened the road past the Two-Mile School: but from Ardagh to Ballyharr chapel the will to words was sapped slowly by the ripening heat of the day. The chapel itself looked the only cool thing under a sun that sent heat down in waves. Joe Jack floundered in the noon tide of it so plainly that anyone but Jack would have seen how he stuck his head up for air every ten yards. Sweat from his bruised feet had seeped through his boots and dust had crusted white as lime on them. He called a halt for a smoke at the chapel gate, put his back to a pillar and all but scraped the coat off his back subsiding down the cool rough stone. Then he lit a fag and snorted smoke down the trumpet nostrils of his broken nose and said: 'Jackeen . . .'

'Well?' asked Jack, the ash plant across his knees, stoking his pipe.

'How's the heart?' asked Joe Jack.

'I'd be shy about asking it,' Jack said.

'Do it sort of flutter when you draw breath?'

'So that's what it was,' said Jack. 'And I thinking 'twas a butterfly I swallyed.'

'Are you serious?' Joe Jack asked, after a pause.

'Oh, the butterfly is gone now.'

'That's something I'm glad to hear,' Joe Jack said, weightily.

'There's a man with a sledge in my temples instead,' said Jack, and Joe Jack rolled over onto his knees.

'Put away that pipe, Jack,' he pleaded. ''Twill suffocate you.'

''Twill suffocate the man with the sledge, you mean.'

'Godelmighty, can't you see that when he stops sledging you stop living, you bloody fool,' cried Joe Jack.

'I'll show him who's gaffer of this job, anyhow.'

'For God's sake have a thought for what I'll do with the dead gaffer.'

'Roll him under a hedge, say a prayer for his soul in the chapel here; then get your own dead feet a lift into Tralee.'

'They're not dead.'

'Then what are you doing on all fours like a donkey?' said Jack, blinking hard. 'Correct yourself before somewan hangs a cart on you.'

'There's a lift on the way here now, but not for me,' said Joe Jack, in real earnest. 'You don't look good, Jackeen; you look like I could fry a rasher on your face.'

'If you had the rasher, you'd be welcome,' said Jack.

A mahogany coloured cob shone with condition down the road towards them. An oak-grained tub trap swayed cradle-easy on good springs after him, with two men and a hefty youth in it. Joe Jack got to a sitting position, and when the cob slung alongside he raised a palm with a shell crust of welts on it.

'Whoa, men,' he said. 'What place are ye bound for?'

'Tralee, at our aise,' said the grey man with the reins.

'I don't like the look of my comrade, so would ye give him the spare seat to Tralee?'

'Take no notice of him, Pats Carty, if you're the sensible man I buy spuds from,' said Jack, without even bothering to blink towards the fresh voice. ''Tis the heat is at him.'

'Yeh, is it you that's there, Jack,' said Carty. 'Devil a bit I see the matter with you.'

Jack stirred: 'There's a man here, Pats, with two dead or dying feet. If your cob can take the weight, you might give him the spare seat he says you have.'

'Either wan or another of ye is welcome, Jack.'

'Not me,' said Jack.

'Nor me,' said Joe Jack. 'But I'd rather you'd take it.'

'Passed unanimous,' said Jack. 'Good-bye, Pats, and thanks for the offer.'

From the chapel up the Firies Cross there was more walk than talk. The heat was too much for all but the bees along the hedges and the butterflies that rose now and again off a hot stone under their feet. Joe Jack doped the pain in a daze of watching the coloured wings flap and skim ahead and flip shut on stones further on. Jack gave his mind to naming birds by their songs. His strong legs, in breeches and stockings, punished the stones with the nails of his boots. The peak of his cap was on his nose to shade his eyes from the hurt of light. Beads of sweat kept falling from Joe Jack's jowls to burst on a khaki shirt as tight as a drumskin on his big-drummer's chest. His step had collapsed into a shuffle that eased the brunt of his great weight to his bruised feet. With a fisted cap he kept mopping a balding skull and a face gritty with dust and stubble. At Firies he broke silence to say he would have to keep an eye out for spring water any-time now, and Jack took the hint.

'Sullivan here in the village have it tapped in barrels,' Jack said. ''Tis a bit off colour from con-finement, they say, but 'tis game ball when you blow the froth off.'

'Never heard of it,' said Joe Jack, heading for the village.

'That's why I mentioned it.'

'How much a barrel is it, tell me?'

'If you drink it off your head in wan go, you can have a barrel for nothing.'

'I'll have a barrel for nothing,' said Joe Jack, mopping the mat of hair at the open neck of his shirt with his cap.

The tiled snug was as cool as a cave. The water wimple in the mirror had ash leaves in it from the tree outside the window. The oak table was lime white from scrubbing and had a blue earthenware jug, with bell heather in it. Froth slobbered over the barman's hand as he put the brimming pint on the table. Joe Jack's tongue licked parched lips loose enough to grin. The barman went to wrench a crown cork off a mineral for Jack. Joe Jack raised the pint to arm's stretch, reverently, above his grin; then drew it down in a slavering relish until it was at lip reach; then he bit out at the brim, like a dog snapping, and drew back his head. The pint sank in gulp after gulp that creamed the glass in gauses of froth as a hissing, unheeded overflow cascaded down the stubbled jowls into the tangle of chest hair. Then suddenly he jerked the empty glass away and yelled loud and snapping as a dog's bark. Still grinning, but in kid-delight now, Joe Jack told the barman: 'Fill it again, my lovely son,' like to a child, as if the savage yell was never his, the rogue black eyes kind enough to own a lolling tongue.

'Let your feet out on the tiles, Joe Jack,' said Jack, still standing, the amber drink in the old hand as out of place as would a toy.

'I'd never get 'em back again,' Joe Jack said, looking at them as if he were talking about a litter of pups.

'Ah, the craythurs won't go far,' encouraged Jack.

'They're headstrong,' said Joe Jack, smiling up at the leaves in the mirror. 'Sometimes they do get too big for their boots.'

''Tis a big world,' Jack reminded.

'But rough underfoot,' said Joe Jack. 'If that road out there was a tar road, I'd let 'em out long ago, but that road out there wasn't made: it was quarried.' Suddenly he saw that Jack had stretched full length on the settle seat under the mirror. 'Oh, for the love of God, Jackeen, rise up out of that,' he implored.

129

'Why so?'

'All you're short to be a corpse is candles.'

Jack laid his cap reverently on his face.

'I can't stand it, I tell you,' Joe Jack appealed.

Jack crossed his hands solemnly on his chest.

'Oh, for the love of God, don't do that,' said Joe Jack.

'S-s-sh,' said Jack. 'That's no way to be carrying on at a wake.'

'Will you sit up, Jack!'

'No.'

'Even that I told you it gives me the creeps!'

'No.'

Joe Jack sulked. Even when Jack took two half-crowns out of a waistcoat pocket and told the barman to keep drawing pints for Joe Jack, the big man sulked. Because Jack went back to the dead man's pose. After three pints in ten minutes, and with a fourth in hand, Joe Jack began to look round the place to avoid looking at the old man. A picture of the 1903 Kerry team caught his eye.

'I suppose you can see this, too,' he said.

'What?'

'The nineteen-hundred-and-three team.'

'Oh, clear I see them,' said Jack from under the cap. 'Oh, God be good to you, Dickeen Fitz, you king in a kingdom of kings.'

'Are you sure you're not dead in earnest?'

'Certain, because Dickeen isn't looking a day older, God rest him, and I am.'

'Maybe you're not dead long enough,' said Joe Jack.

'There they all are now taking the pitch in their

130

prime. Dickeen, Paddy Dillon, Austin Stack, Champion Sullivan, Dinny Kissane, Big Jack Myers. Fine, I can see them now skying balls to the sun and rising half way to meet them coming back.'

Still in his dead man's stretch, Jack's voice gloried out from under the cap, and Joe was stung into shouting: 'There was good men since.'

'Good men, Joe Jack, but never as good as the men I'm with now. Rocks in play for gallant men to break on, and men to laugh with and drink with when the waves were spent. Oh, God be with ye, the men I'm with now.'

'Was Paul Russell as good as any of them?' said Joe Jack.

'Was any son as good as his father?'

'Was any wan of them as good as Joe Barrett, or Con Brosnan, or John Joe Sheehy, or Miko Boyle, or Purty Landers, or Timmie Leary, or Jackie Lyne?'

'Good men all, but never as good as the men I'm with now. Fit to carry the game you shaped for them, Dickeen boy, but no more than that, Dickeen, you king in a kingdom of kings.'

'Time stopped for their last whistle, I suppose.'

'Don't mind him, Dickeen.'

'Did you see Russell in '32 at Croke Park driving a goal from fifty yards?'

'Don't mind him, Dickeen, carry on with your game.'

Joe Jack lunged past the table and towered up into a rage over Jack's dead man's stretch.

'Will you listen, Jackeen!'

'We won't listen, Dickeen,' Jack gloated under

the cap.

'Then you can go the rest of the way with Dickeen,' said Joe Jack, lunging for the snug door.

'I knew him well,' Jack called to a Joe Jack blundering about in the open bar.

'Give up the ghost and ye'll be shaking hands!'

'Go, if you're going.'

'Give up the ghost, Jackeen!'

'Go to the boneyard, Joe Jack!'

And the whole house shook as Joe Jack banged the front door after him. Rage carried him a quarter mile at a jog-trot before his feet brought him to his senses. He fell on his rump onto the road with pain. Before him the road leaned up against the sky like a ladder against a blue-washed dome. It felt the easiest-thing to roll back half a dozen miles into unconsciousness or sleep, but sweat came on tap to sear sleep off his lids. The hurt to his eyes put him thinking of Jack, and, when he looked back, Jack was striding after him, touching the road with the ash plant. When Jack was near enough to hear the boy's teeth-whistle from his old man's mouth, Joe Jack rose and lunged ahead in a shuffle of desperation that was the only way he knew how of getting the better of his bruised feet. Then he flopped back on the road again, mopped head, face and chest with the cap until the teeth-whistle slit the hush of heat and he had to heave ahead again, his power robbed of dignity in that lunatic shuffle. On top of the mountain he fell face down under the blue dome into the coolness of long grass by the road-side. When Jack laboured up the last rise Joe Jack found he was without the will to stir more than an eye his way. Jack stood mid-road on the mountain top, with the plant in his hand, like a blind shepherd under a Bible sky. He cocked an ear to right and left; then, after a pause, said:

'Joe Jack.'

Joe Jack neither moved nor spoke. The hush hummed with heat. Larksong ran out of the sky like grain through a rent in an apron. 'Joe Jack, are you all right?' Joe Jack began to relish the situation. 'Joe Jack, are you all right? Are you all right, I said? . . . You must be near, because I could hear you ahead up to now. . . . Joe Jack, show a sign anyhow. . . . Joe Jack!'

'Stand in off the road before the larks do more than sing on top of you,' said Joe Jack, drowsily.

'You had me worried,' said Jack, at his ease now.

'I could see that,' said Joe Jack.

'Worried I might have to run all the way back for a gun to take you out of pain.'

'I got to the top of the mountain before you, all the same.'

'There's a view for you,' said Jack. 'The vale of Tralee. Do you want me to see it for you, you boneyard stray?'

'A postcard,' said Joe Jack, feeling with his face for cooler grass. 'I think I'll post it to John Joe Sheehey to hold the match until we hit Tralee this day week.'

'Here, I'll sit with you until the end comes,' said Jack.

He walked in the direction of Joe Jack's voice until he could see where he was. Then he lay in the dead man's stretch on the grass beside him and

133

retired under the cap. Neither was able to say afterward who went to sleep first, but Jack was first to awaken. To bring Joe Jack back he had to fist his ribs till he sounded like a barrel being tapped. 'I was dreaming I was in bed,' said Joe Jack.

''Tis time to get up now,' said Jack. 'What time do it look like?' Joe Jack said: 'Two by the sky.' Jack said: 'An hour to the match and the hill down with us. Come on.'

But it was Joe Jack who was first on his feet, to make ground in a kind of second wind he was afraid to mention lest it leave him. The downhill going changed the pressure on his feet but he wore sweat like a caul. When the more sprightly shuffle sprawled again into new fatigue the firm step of Jack got on his nerves and he began to hulk ahead once more. Then he rounded another bend and cried out with the full of his lungs and shambling, stumbling, falling, rising, always shouting, he hulked downhill. Jack pulled up between strides and yelled at the top of his voice: 'Joe Jack!' Then, well ahead and below him, Joe Jack began to laugh great gusts of laughter that tossed a gibberish of words about like corks on a wave. Jack thought he had gone out of his mind. With the ash plant held straight out he began to run blindly down into booming chesty phlegmy laughter until the ash was whipped out of his hand and he hit the hulk of Joe Jack's bone and muscle the way he would a moss-plushed wall. Shaken and winded he blinked up into the porter-smelling laughter from the mouth of Joe Jack.

'What's the matter, Joe Jack?'

For answer Joe Jack lashed the road with the ash.

'Can't you see as far as the ground, Jackeen? Look!' Jack stooped and was blinking at a pair of broad, flat feet, boning red through holes in smelling socks.

'They're like something a flood would lave on a mud-bank, Joe Jack.'

'Only they're nayther dead nor drowned,' raved Joe Jack.

'They're on the tar road, man, no more stones, smooth as a dance floor, man, whistle a tune and I'll dance.'

'Wind's gone,' said Jack.

Then Joe Jack's high glee went out like a light. 'Hey, hold on there, oldtimer,' he said. Jack's face had gone from red to a murky puce. His breathing came in jerks. 'Give us the ash, Joe Jack,' he said. Joe Jack put the plant in his fist and took him by the arm. 'Aisy now, sit on the ditch, Jack.' Jack shook the hand off. 'That run winded me, that's all,' he said, but he staggered as he spoke. When he tapped with the ash towards the ditch his legs trembled. He leaned against the ditch. 'Sledge gone. Butterfly back,' he said. Joe Jack slung his boots to hang fore and aft by the laces from his shoulders. 'That's what you get from drinking minerals,' he told Jack. 'Puts wind around the ticker. A few belches and you'll be game ball.' Jack blinked at the sky, as if listening to count heart-beats. Joe Jack's battered face had a death-bed concern that matched his feelings perfectly. Jack licked blue lips with a dry tongue, gasping. He slid down the ditch into a sitting position. Joe Jack began to massage his face as gently as huge hands and hard palms would let him, and Jack felt a benefit or was too weak to

135

protest.

'Come on, Jackeen, we have a match to ketch. Two downhill miles and a pint that you'll buy for Joe Jack. Tay for Jack this time, no minerals, no arguments until after the match; then more pints for Joe Jack. . . . Ah, sure we're game ball again. . . .'

The gentle man-handling brought colour back to Jack's face. He raised a hand to push Joe Jack's palms away.

'Dickeen was asking for you, Joe,' he said.

Joe Jack stood over him with his hands hanging like a bear waiting for trainer's orders. He lit a fag and sucked it limp with one long drag. Not sure of how to bring Jack further towards the land of the living, he decided on singing.

'Good heart, Joe Jack,' said Jack. ''Tis strange, but you never sounded better than worse till now.' He began to help himself up along the ditch with his arms. 'If I can stand I'll walk,' he said. He got as far as standing, rested for a moment; then heaved himself onto the roadway, swayed, steadied up and began to walk and tap with the ash, but slowly. 'Come on, do you want to keep me all day on the road?' he asked Joe Jack and Joe Jack came up and fell into step. And anyone but Jack would have seen the blood stains Joe Jack left on the crust of the road until the sun baked the wounds on his feet.

Joe Jack was going better without the boots, but he pretended distress in hundred-yard intervals to give Jack a breather without having to admit that he needed it. Within the hour Tralee opened its eyes to the shuffling bear of a man on bruised feet in holed socks and boots dangling by the laces from his shoulder, mopping a balding head with a fisted cap: and beside him a man whose face sagged grey in near-exhaustion, touching the road with an ash plant, trying to persuade breeched and stockinged legs to keep his nailed boots moving. Joe Jack's trumpet nostrils smelled porter through pub doors, saw coolness and quietness through pub windows but he was bent on knocking up the first chemist to get a doctor's draught for Jack.

The claret inside cut glass on the chemist's counter boiled Joe Jack's thirst into spittle again, but Jack got his draught, belched, broke wind, and said: 'Will you fix that fellah's feet so they'll fit his boots again and not be making a show of me.'

While the chemist patched his feet with lint, plaster and bandage, Joe Jack cut the uppers of his boots into sandal strips with a scalpel he took off a shelf. Then the chemist saw what he was at and howled at the indignity to the gleaming instrument, but the damage was done, and Joe Jack was able to ease his feet into the gartered brogues. Jack led off the main beat for a bite and a sup before they faced the Austin Stack Park.

'Better get some sort of Christian look about you before we face anywan we know,' he explained.

'You have the advantage on me, Jack; you can't see yourself,' Joe Jack growled.

Jack went upstairs in Con Clifford's for tea and a plate of ham, while Joe Jack stayed downstairs for porter and sandwiches. When Jack tapped his way down with the ash, he found Joe Jack well gone in liquor and reluctant to leave without a few more pints, but the clock was against him.

137

They bought tickets at the gate to the ground and tickets on the ground to the stand. They found there was no room on the stand, and hundreds of the faces that tiered all the way to the roof at the back came alive in cheers and shouting the minute the pair came in sight.

'Sound man, Joe Jack! . . . My life on you, Jack, with your twenty-wan miles when you should be at home with your rosary beads!'

'Ould Carty blew the gaff,' said Jack, in disgust, but Joe Jack revelled in the reception, the broken face fixed in a grin. Jack turned towards a white-lined pitch that gleamed green between lime-washed goalposts, but Joe Jack turned his back on it as home-town faces in the stand began to call: 'Speech, Joe Jack, speech!' Joe Jack took the cap off, tore at the tufts of hair with a huge hand, and every face known and unknown above him hissed 'S-s-s-sh' and called 'Order! Order.' Joe Jack cleared his throat.

'We done it anyhow!' he said, and was cheered to the echo. 'The road was as hot as the hobs of hell!' he said, and they cheered again, and from there on they cheered every statement.

'My butty, Jack here, walked his sight back. . . . He seen Son Leary at Innisfallen off the top of Madam's Height.'

Jack's quick wheel caught the cheer leaders off guard: 'In hundreds wan, two, three and four, come away, Joe Jack, and say no more,' he said, for the loudest cheer of the lot. But Joe Jack was on cue.

'From Sullivan's snug in Firies he saw all the

way back to nineteen hunderth and three,' he said, and the cheers and laughter were his again. 'He wanted me to go back with him, but the ould feet wouldn't let me.'

Every face on the stand was laughing at him and with him now, and he gloried in his moment. Jack was straining to be away.

'Jack left me to go back there himself, and, God's truth, he nearly forgot to come back to me again.'

The tiers of faces were straining down to hear and Joe Jack obliged by bellowing up at them:

'I got corns in hindquarters from sitting on the road!'

The faces laughed louder, swayed and leaned nearer, and Joe Jack gloried on.

'There was the man called Carty with the trap—he—'

But the teams had burst into colour onto the pitch behind him and the faces forsook him on the instant.

'There was the man called Carty—' he tried again, but his bull-powerful bellow was drowned in cheers that broke over him in a wave onto the pitch.

'There was the man—' he insisted, but not a face turned his way.

'There was—'

The waves of sound quenched the words at his lips. His fighter's face looked punch drunk. Jack felt for his arm and gripped it.

'Come on, Joe Jack!' he shouted in the big man's ear, but he had to tug several times before

139

he could get him headed toward the wall that bounded the pitch.

'I must see that match!' Jack shouted.

'If I have to walk it,' said Joe Jack. And no one, not even himself, was aware of what he had said.

For full deails of all Poolbeg Press books
in print, write to

Poolbeg Press,
Knocksedan House,
Swords, Co. Dublin.
Telephone 401133.
Telex 24639.

A LIFE OF HER OWN

Maeve Kelly

". . . richly human and perceptive and highly recommended to all those who have not yet had the pleasure." *Sunday Press.*

0 905169 04 2/110x178mm/144pp/Paper/£1.50

A GIFT HORSE

Kate Cruise O'Brien

"I am going to stick my neck out, and possibly make a fool of myself. It is a thing that even the most conservative critic has to do once or twice in a lifetime. It is unarguable that Kate Cruise O'Brien's stories reveal a very special talent, but each time I reread them, and I have now read them three times, I get the feeling that they reveal something much more — a seed of genius."
Sunday Press

"These stories slide themselves into the best of company and are rewardingly full of promise."
Irish Press

0 905169 08 5/184x112mm/128pp/Paper/£1.50